THE HUNT

Also by James Powell:

DEATHWIND
THE MALPAIS RIDER

THE HUNT

JAMES POWELL

DOUBLEDAY & COMPANY, INC.
GARDEN CITY, NEW YORK
1982

All of the characters in this book are fictitious, and any resemblance to actual persons, living or dead, is purely coincidental.

Library of Congress Cataloging in Publication Data

Powell, James.
The hunt.

(Double D western)
I. Title.
PS3566.O832H8   813'.54
ISBN 0-385-17994-4   AACR2
Library of Congress Catalog Card Number 81-43450

THE HUNT

PROLOGUE

1

There was no record of the fact, of course, but the bear was born right there in the basin, toward the end of January 1879. A rare single offspring among grizzlies, he was born of an old sow that had always before given birth to no fewer than twins but was probably lucky this time to have delivered even the one. He was a tiny thing—weighing little more than a pound and stretching but a meager ten inches in length—and he was naked. But this didn't matter; all grizzlies were tiny and mostly naked at birth. It had no bearing on how large or impressively coated he would eventually become.

By spring, when the old sow emerged from her winter den, the cub was yet to weigh three pounds. This was just about normal.

He followed his mamma throughout spring and summer and, although still a dependent cub, was healthy and fat when fall once again came upon the land. The sow, on the other hand, had not prospered. Her age telling on her now like never before, she was not in as good a shape as she should have been. She sought her den early that year, and the following spring, when the cub emerged from the den, the sow did not. The old bear's heart had simply slowed till it stopped; she had died just two days before the cub poked its head outside the den.

For two days more the little fellow stayed close by, whimpering pitifully. Now and then he came to the den to poke and paw at his mother's body, but at last he realized that there would be no response, and early the third morning he waddled off into the nearby timber to begin spending his yearling year alone.

His first problem, of course, was food. It was yet early spring, there in the San Juan Mountains of southern Colorado, and snow remained on the north-facing slopes all around him. Instinctively he headed for the south slopes. For over a month he lived mostly on the early-greening grass he found there, on mice and ground squirrels and chipmunks dug from their own dens in and beneath rotting logs, on roots or whatever else he could find that seemed edible and would also fit into his mouth. Later on, as summer proceeded, there were berries, ants, honey, and finally the fresh carcass of a deer killed by some other predator and left unattended for a later meal. He liked the taste of meat best of all, but he was not yet an accomplished killer. He had to take what he could get.

By fall he had done pretty well. He had grown fat and sleek and was just beginning to put on a winter coat. Already, too, he was strikingly colored, even for a grizzly. Called "white" or "yellow" bears by some, "silvertips" by others, few grizzlies achieved quite the coloration of this bear. Darker than most even in the body, his lower legs were almost solid black, and his coat over his sides, back, and shoulders was so tipped with light hairs against a darker base that in the right light he looked like pure, shimmering silver. This would dull some over the winter and with the years, but even so he would remain forever conspicuous even among his own kind.

Not that he came in contact with his own kind all that much that summer; generally he did not. An early lesson he had to learn was that other grizzlies, particularly the older males, established their own territories and were not inclined to share them with yearling cubs. Whenever he saw their claw marks scratched well up on the pines all around, thus marking a territory already taken, he knew to wander on. The she-bears wanted no part of him either, especially if they had at their sides their own cubs. And on his own he instinctively disdained contact with the many cinnamon or black bears he saw. These were *not* his kind, there could be no confusion about that. To be a grizzly was to stand alone most of the time, and this bear was a grizzly with no inclination to be anything else.

He made his den that winter and emerged the next spring to find catkins forming on the aspen and willows, and green grass just beginning to grow on the south slopes. He roamed the basin, the mountains all around, the rivers from the East Fork of the San Juan in the north to the upper flowings of the Navajo and Little Navajo down near the New Mexico line. He learned to catch trout in the streams; he worked and worked at hunting and finally downed his first major kill, a young doe that made unbelievably good eating. He saw birds and other animals—from wild turkey and jays and the incessantly chattering, scolding magpies, to chipmunks, squirrels, skunks, porcupines, rabbits, deer, elk, black bears, and mountain lions—and he did not step aside for any of them. He saw other grizzlies and he *did* step aside, but only because he was not yet ready to fight for a territory. When the time came, things would be different, of course.

The aspen turned yellow and the oak brush red; another winter drew near. Once again he made his den. Another year passed, then yet another. The spring that he was four he mated with a young she-bear that somehow had not been claimed by a larger male. The mating was a short, somewhat volatile affair, carrying with it no permanent attachment whatsoever—as is the case with grizzlies, for they are almost arrogantly promiscuous.

Later on, in summer, he once again wandered the mountains far and wide; by late fall, however, he was back in the basin. He had not truly established this as *his* territory yet, but for him there never was any doubt where home was and returning to the basin each year in the fall already seemed the only natural thing to do. It was a pattern he was destined never to change.

He was not challenged there until the following spring when he had his first fight with another somewhat immature bear of similar size out to indulge in his own first territorial dispute. The battle was no contest from the start. When it was over the silver bear was one-of-one as a fighter and had hardly a scratch to show for the other bear's effort. He was just beginning to experience the prowess that was his to come.

It was an extraordinarily isolated area, the basin and this portion of the San Juan Mountains; and thus he was somehow in his sixth year before his next important milestone was reached, when he experienced his first face-to-face confrontation with man. Although he had seen these strange creatures before, it had been only from a distance and he had instinctively chosen to keep it that way. On this occasion, however, he had wandered farther westward than usual, to the confluence of the Blanco and San Juan rivers, and near dark one evening was splashing about in the stream after trout when a loud crack sounded nearby. Something whistled past. A two-legged form appeared on the bank—a Ute Indian whose lodge was likely not far away. The Indian was a poor shot, fortunately for the bear, who immediately left the stream and shuffled off into the brush. He had not learned much about guns and hunters yet, but he did know danger when he smelled it and that two-legged being who-stood-like-a-bear-but-was-not-a-bear was danger personified. But he was not hit, there was no pain, and thus he did not react with the characteristically violent temper of his kind. Wisely, he fled rather than attack, and it would never be known who was the more lucky that day, the Indian or the bear. It should have been more disturbing than it was to both of them.

Naturally it was not to be the bear's last contact with man. Things were changing rapidly now in the San Juans, and over the next few years he would encounter these suspicious creatures more and more; he would see them on foot and riding horseback; he would hear with alarm the startling boom those curious sticks they carried could make—usually from a safe distance—and he would even observe firsthand the quick death the deadly boom sticks could bring to other animals. This should have been frightening to him, but the silver bear was like the Indians about such things: His was not to fear, his was the wary caution of survival. Man was something very special in a forest where the grizzly otherwise reigned supreme. Whether it be from intelligence or instinct, the silver bear knew this and kept his distance. But he was not afraid.

Nevertheless, a policy of complete avoidance was something that could only grow harder and harder to exercise. Not only were the number of men increasing now, but at the lower elevations, at least, they were bringing more and more of a certain strange animal with them: Four-legged, docile-eyed creatures that grazed like elk but were not elk, neither as wild nor as smart; creatures that grew large and fat and were loaded with good red meat, but which were also slow and not at all adept at getting away from an enterprising lion or bear.

The silver bear was of a species that had been around for a long, long time; a species that dated back to the mastodons and saber-toothed tigers; a species much quicker to learn to adapt than those that had gone before him and failed all those eons ago to survive.

Till now such adaptability had always been a strength; the bear had no way of knowing that it could also lead him into outlawry. He had grown to love deer and elk flesh like nothing else he had found to eat, but he was soon to find that these new creatures could yield even better fare yet, if for no other reason than there was so much more of them and they were so much easier to get.

At first he was hesitant, cautious. He had learned to be wary whenever man and his animals were encountered. He did not go hunting for trouble.

Inevitably, it came anyway.

The first beef he ever tasted wasn't even of his own kill; it was from a fresh carcass he came across, a lion's doing. The tawny culprit was in fact surprised as it fed and was chased away, snarling and spitting and knowing better than to match itself with the bear. The big grizzly settled down to feast. The meat was good, a taste he acquired instantly and of which he would never be rid. In no time he had taken to killing his own.

He was in his eighth year then. It was but a year later when he was shot for the first time by an angry stockman's boom stick—and in a resultant rage killed his first man.

It was only the beginning.

2

By the spring of 1895, in his sixteenth year, he was a full-blown legend still going strong. His fame (infamy if you wish) had grown, spreading from Colorado's San Juan Mountains not only to adjoining states and territories, but all the way to the East Coast and beyond. He was billed as a great cattle- and man-killing grizzly, perhaps a ton in weight (somewhat exaggerated) and a full eleven feet in height (only slightly exaggerated); a bear that had defied all reputedly to slay and consume perhaps a thousand head of cattle, uncounted sheep, no less than two dozen horses, and to have killed at least three men. He was feared, revered, hated, and written about. He was pursued and hunted both unmercifully and desperately. He was both villain and hero, the former for his many haughty misdeeds, the latter for his unbelievable ability to avoid being brought to ground. He had three different one-thousand-dollar rewards on his head. Almost every local hunter, trapper, stockman, cowboy, and herder had had a hand at tracking him down and trying to kill him. He had been shot at and hit, caught in traps, hounded, and even cornered by dogs. Always he escaped.

A newspaperman had come all the way from New York City to write about him. Captivated by the tales he was told, the man had written extensively. His stories had been printed not only at home but abroad. To hunters everywhere, the bear was a grand prize, among the most coveted of them all. He was the stuff that Western legends were made of—exaggerated, perhaps, for that's storytelling—but there was no denying that he was real.

He came to have more than one name. Mexicans in the area told endless, frightening stories about *El Oso de Muerte*—The Bear of Death; Indians spoke reverently of what was to them a true Spirit Bear; Anglos, in pragmatic respect, called him simply Old Tuffy. But to all of them he was huge and he was silver. He was held in awe. In a day and time when his kind were disappearing with frightening rapidity in the face of man's encroachment throughout his domain, the silver bear as much as owned the lower San Juans.

CHAPTER 1
THE HUNTERS

1

The nearest town of any consequence to all of this sprawled peacefully along the banks of the San Juan River, on the periphery of the big bear's range. It was primarily a sawmill town, first platted by the government in 1880 near the site of an early-day military garrison. The garrison, however, had shortly thereafter been removed to a spot sixty miles or so to the west, near Durango, leaving the town to capitalize as best it could on the vast timber-producing resources that surrounded it, a certain sure-to-increase amount of stock raising, and a yet to be fully appreciated cluster of hot mineral springs to which health seekers would someday flock in great numbers.

In recent years sawmill production had faltered somewhat, partly because much of the most easily harvested timber had already been cut, but as much as anything because of the unsettled economy the nation—and Colorado—had been fretting with ever since what had come to be called the Panic of 1893. Fact was, Colorado had been particularly hard hit. Silver prices had plummeted, the cattle industry still had not fully recovered from the disastrous late eighties and early nineties, and the state's one hale and hearty pillar of industry—the Cripple Creek goldfields—had recently been beset with labor problems and even violence.

In short, times were troubled and there were not many who went unaffected. What recovery there was could only be termed cautious, and it was a time of change for almost everyone.

Especially caught up in the situation were those persistent survivors still trying to make it as cattle raisers in the face of everything from disastrous weather extremes to much moderated beef prices, the rapid encroachment of homesteading farmers, and, of course, sheep. In the cowmen's case, many of the large conglomerate ownerships had long since been torn asunder, and a new breed of smaller operators had surfaced. Fences were going up in profusion, new breeds of cattle were replacing the hardy but skinny Texas Longhorn, new ways were being sought to keep stock alive and productive overwinter, and virtual wars were being fought with sheepmen over ranges already fully stocked with cows but to which the newcomers believed they had as much right as anyone else.

Not everyone was caught up in the worst of this, but one aspiring example of the new breed was Gil Whitney, a dark-haired young rancher who rode into town one sunny afternoon in May and dismounted in front of Bud Sampson's general store. It was his first time in town in over three weeks, and as he tied his horse to the rail in front of the store he could hardly be expected to overlook a particular commotion in the street, up near the hotel, a block away.

Bud Sampson stood on the walk outside, watching.

"Some mess, huh, Gil," he commented with a slow wag of his shaggy head.

"I dunno," Gil said, stepping onto the walk in a single, easy motion. "What *is* it?"

"You won't believe it. I don't, and I know what I'm looking at."

"Try me."

Three sturdy Studebaker wagons, each with two-horse teams hitched on, two large surreys, a buckboard, and a small crowd of people standing around claimed the scene. A pair of Ute Indians from the reservation south and west of town also stood nearby and appeared greatly amused by the air of confusion that seemed to prevail.

"A hunting party," the storekeeper said. "Foreigners and Easterners, come to get the bear. Can you believe that? All the way from London, England, and New York City—thinking they got a chance to bring in Old Tuffy. Boy oh boy!"

"You're right. I don't believe it."

The other man grinned. "Well, it's interesting that you come riding in, 'cause I been thinking about you and there's even more you won't believe where that come from. Guess who was to be their guide on the 'expedition,' as they call it?"

"Guide?" Gil frowned. There was only one person who came immediately to mind. "I hope you're kidding me, Bud. Either that or I hope my guess is wrong."

"Nope," the storekeeper said. "Not a chance, either way. Dawson Riddle—'The one man who knows it all about the bear.' The one and only."

He quoted, more than a bit sarcastically, from one of the now famous pieces written by that New York newspaperman a year ago, in which Dawson Riddle had figured almost as prominently as the bear—which fact was greeted in turn by most locals who knew the man as nothing more than some kind of preposterous joke. To be sure, Riddle was something of a hunter and guide. And he did claim openly to have spent the last few years, off and on, in pursuit of the bear. But to have successfully cast himself in the role of the bear's chief nemesis the way he had with that newspaper fellow brought only wry smiles and quick utterances of disdain from those who really knew the score.

Dawson Riddle might have hunted the bear; he might even have seen the animal . . . once, maybe twice. But much better hunters than he had taken their try at Old Tuffy and failed. Dawson Riddle was *not* the best man around to go after a prize such as San Juan country's great silver-coated grizzly. Anyone could tell you that.

Gil shook his head. "So what's going on now? Where's Dawson?"

"Well, that's the main problem," Sampson said. "Apparently this crowd arrived on the train in Durango a week ago. They spent the time it took to buy up all those wagons and horses and stuff you see there and then headed for here. According to them, they had communicated several times with Dawson beginning sometime last fall and had it all arranged for him to guide them on a big hunt for the bear this spring as soon as the snow was off down low. Trouble is, they showed up on schedule at his place west of town this morning, only to find him drunk as a skunk and in no shape to guide anybody anywhere. They had some sort of fuss over it and straightaway fired him from the job. Now they're here, looking for a new guide and a place to set up camp. They're not one damn bit happy that nobody's yet come forward to bail them out of their predicament, either."

Gil whistled softly. "Sounds like some hunting party. What are they—royalty or just rich?"

Sampson smiled. "Some of both, I reckon. I was over there a few minutes ago and found out some of it. There's six of them altogether—four from England, two from New York. The two from New York are friends of that newspaper fellow who wrote the story, if that tells you anything. So are the other four, only they're some kind of English aristocrats—you know, dukes or barons or some such. At least two of 'em are. That's another problem with this bunch of bear hunters: Half of 'em are women!"

Gil switched his gaze back up the street. "Well, now, that *is* hard to believe. Are you sure?"

"I saw 'em myself. Three men, three women—one of which is a real looker, let me tell you." He stopped then to squint at a skeptical-looking Gil. "You still don't believe me, huh? Well, go on over and have a look for yourself. You'll see."

Gil studied the group for a moment more. "I think I'll take your word for it."

But Sampson, seemingly serious about what he'd just said, persisted. "It might be worth your while, Gil. Damn well it might."

"How do you figure that?"

"Well, for one thing, *you* could guide 'em. Now, come on, don't look at me like that. You know Old Tuffy's country as well as anyone around, and you've hunted him. You and I both know they could do a lot worse than you."

Gil stared at him. "Why would I want to get mixed up in something like that? You know I don't have time to—"

Sampson didn't let him finish. "They're paying good money, boy. At least what they say they offered Dawson was good."

Gil straightened slightly. "How much?"

"A thousand straight out and half the bounty money if the bear's killed by a member of the party."

Gil whistled. "Good money, all right. No question about that."

"And you could use it, too, couldn't you? You and that Echo Canyon ranch of yours. You know you could."

Gil had to nod yes to this. Ever since he had acquired his patent to that small homestead of his in Echo Canyon three years ago, he had had an uphill struggle just to hang on. The first summer he'd repaired, then built on to an existing house—a three-room log cabin he'd now expanded to six rooms—and had begun to build a fence around the place. The second summer he'd started a barn and corrals and had finished most of the fence. This summer he intended to finish the barn and corrals. But he had started with barely fifty head of cattle and that was not even close to being enough to make a real go of it with. Worse, even with the calves that had been born and kept in the interim, the herd's numbers had dwindled rather than grown. A fourth of its original members had either starved or frozen to death over the first two winters. Half a dozen more had been killed by lion and bear, while a dozen others had disappeared for no telling what reasons over the past winter and Gil had no idea if he would ever see any of these again. It would help some if he could feed them overwinter and he wanted to cultivate his meadows to grow hay for that purpose. But he lacked the money for seed and equipment, and so far this was only a dream he had. He had worked part time at the sawmill, raised a garden, and killed wild game for meat, and thus had done at least an adequate job of surviving. But as far as his ranching operation went, he seemed to be losing ground rather than gaining, and if ever anybody could use a thousand dollars and more, Gil Whitney could. Bud Sampson knew that as well as anybody.

"Well?" the storekeeper persisted anyway.

"You know I can use the money, Bud. But taking a bunch of silly tenderfeet out on a hunt for Old Tuffy isn't my idea of the way to make it. Not when the best hunters in Colorado and New Mexico have already tried and failed and I know it's likely hopeless. And I certainly wouldn't do it with women along. No way I'd let myself in for that!"

Sampson wagged his head sadly. "Somehow, I was afraid you'd say something like that."

Once again Gil eyed him suspiciously. "But you gave them my name anyway. Is that right?"

"Well, yes, I did. I figured you could use the money, so by golly, I sure did!"

Gil sighed. It was hard to be mad at Sampson; the man was only trying to help. "Well, no harm done, I guess. I can always say no, if they ask." He put his hand on the storekeeper's shoulder. "Enough of that anyway, Bud. Right now, I need some things from your store. I hope my credit's still good. Is it?"

Bud Sampson stared at him. "Now, you see there! That's what happens. A man turns his nose up at a job that could make him some real money and the very next thing asks for credit at my store! Boy oh boy! Well, come on, let's go inside. . . . And by the way, when you're through here, June Greer told me next time I saw you to make sure you stop by her ma's cafe. You do it, too. I don't want that young gal mad at me 'cause I didn't tell you, you hear?"

2

Gil finished his business at Sampson's, then led his horse on up the street toward Helen Greer's restaurant. Stopping half a block short of the commotion still going on in the street, he once again tied up to the rail and stepped onto the walk.

There was only one other customer inside the restaurant at that hour, and that individual sat at the counter contemplating a cup of no longer steaming-hot coffee. June's mother, Helen Greer, stood across the counter from him, apparently having stopped whatever else she had been doing for a chat. The man was Gil's closest neighbor, a rancher named Garst Cunningham.

"Afternoon, ma'am, Garst," Gil said, removing his hat and coming up to take a stool next to Cunningham.

Helen Greer, a slender, attractive lady of about fifty, smiled politely. Cunningham nodded, perhaps a bit uncomfortably. It was no secret that both Garst and Gil were interested in June Greer, and probably because of that they were not the fastest of friends. It was no secret, either, which one of them Mrs. Greer favored for her daughter. Garst Cunningham was at least a moderately successful cattleman; Gil had lost over half of his original herd in two years of trying and was right now anything but the most attractive suitor—at least from a mother's point of view.

Still, to give her credit, the woman had never openly interfered in the situation. Her feelings were known, especially to the girl, and that is where she had always left them. She said to Gil, "We haven't seen you in weeks, it seems. I guess you've been busy."

"Yes, ma'am," Gil said, knowing he shouldn't need to explain but doing so anyway. "The snow's all but gone down low now, and I've had a lot of spring work to get done."

The woman once again smiled politely, then cast a somewhat apologetic glance toward Cunningham. "June's out back, but she should be back any minute now. Would you like some coffee, Gil? Something to eat?"

"Just coffee," he said, then watched as she filled a cup and set it in front of him before quickly disappearing into the kitchen. He turned to Cunningham. "How're things on your side of the hill, Garst?"

The other man wagged his head. His place was one ridge over from Gil's, in the direction of town. He was at least ten years older than Gil, fifteen pounds heavier, and an inch taller. He was ruddy-cheeked and fair where Gil was dark and gray-eyed; he was also mustachioed and not at all bad-looking. "Tolerable, I reckon," he said. "Be branding calves next week—those the bears haven't got, anyway."

"Bears?" Gil was a little surprised. "You're having trouble with bears already?"

The other man nodded. "Damn right, I am. They started coming out early this spring and haven't let me alone since. Course, I suspect Old Tuffy's at the heart of it. Nothing that old hellion loves better than calf meat, damn his hide."

"Have you seen him?"

"Naw, nobody ever sees the old bastard. He's too slick for that.

We've seen his tracks, though. There's no mistaking those paw prints of his—back foot seven inches across and a foot long; claw marks showing well ahead of the front toes; three toes missing on his right front foot, two on the left. No bear I know of leaves a track that size or with its front feet so mangled up by traps."

Gil fingered his coffee cup thoughtfully. "You've found Tuffy's tracks around calf kills this spring?" He knew the tracks well and could not dispute the description, but he was vaguely disturbed— always had been—about the number and frequency of kills attributed to the big grizzly. As was common with such stories, the bear would have to have been in a dozen places at once to do even one fourth of the damage attributed to him.

Cunningham nodded. "More'n once . . . although you know as well as I that we never even find most kills—especially the ones that smart old bastard's made. Dammit, I sure wish someone'd bring him down. It'd save me fifty head of cattle a year, at least."

Gil smiled. Another exaggeration, of course—although perhaps not as great a one as some people might think. A big bear like that had a hell of an appetite, no question about it. And no telling how many kills were made that, for one reason or another, the animal never finished feeding upon. But fifty a year for every rancher who claimed that many was more guilt than even Old Tuffy ought to be saddled with; Gil would be among the first to admit that and if pressed to it, probably so would Garst Cunningham.

"Well, Garst, maybe someone'll get him this year. Who knows, maybe even that bunch out in the street has a chance."

Cunningham looked up. "Are they still out there?" Then he wagged his head scornfully. "Yeah, they'll kill the bear, all right— right after I'm elected President of the country, the price of silver jumps to two dollars an ounce, and cattle go to a hundred a head. Yes sir, that's when such a bunch of dudes as them will kill the bear!"

Gil smiled again but didn't say anything as Mrs. Greer came back in from the kitchen and said, "I'm sure June will be here soon. More coffee, either of you?"

Cunningham looked suddenly uncomfortable, as if he'd already waited long enough. "Thanks, ma'am, but I reckon I'd better be going. I wanta see what's become of that bunch of so-called bear hunters out there, then I've gotta get on back to the ranch." But he did little to hide his irritation with Gil as he reached over and picked up his hat from an adjacent stool. He said as he rose, "Keep an eye out for the bear, Whitney. Never can tell when he'll run out of good fat calves over at my place and start going after some of those skinny ones over at yours." He laughed humorlessly as he turned to leave.

Gil frowned but let it drop, and Cunningham went through the front door only moments before Gil heard the kitchen doors swing open behind him. He turned just in time to see June and her mother pass each other, the latter on her way back into the kitchen.

When they were alone, the girl said, "Hello, Gil. I thought maybe you'd forgotten I was alive."

She was the kind of simply pretty girl many men will choose over one that is more strikingly beautiful: All softly molded and even-featured, from eyes to nose to mouth to chin, with few flaws of complexion and with femininity abounding at every curve of her slender but not too slender body. Her hair was light brown, with but the softest tinge of red; and although her hairline was a mite too high it detracted little from her prettiness. She was a bit taller than average for a girl, but Gil did not think she was too tall. Her teeth were even and white, her smile engaging, and her voice was neither husky and low nor high and unevenly pitched like so many of the other girls around. When she laughed it was a pretty sound and when she frowned the fact was worth making note of. She was everything Gil thought he wanted in a girl, which very much made him afraid even to dream that she could ever really be his.

He made an effort to smile, despite a keen awareness that she still had not. "It's been a tough winter, June. I come in as often as I can."

"Garst comes in every week," she said, almost as if trying not to make the point any more obvious than it already was. "Your place is only a couple of miles beyond his."

Gil tensed slightly. "Then he should be ahead of me in the race. Is that it? Because he has a full-fledged crew and I have only one old man to help me, and he can come in more often, he should be leading the field . . . is that what you're saying?"

Her eyes were of a sudden very, very gray. "There is no race, Gil, no field. Not unless you choose not to run. I stayed out back all the time Garst was here just now; I waited till he left to come in. Did you know that?"

Gil tried not to show his surprise at this revelation. "No," he said slowly, "but I think maybe *he* did. He didn't leave in the merriest of moods, now that I think about it."

Finally she smiled just a bit, then came around the counter to sit on the stool next to him. "Well, I'm glad you came, anyway. I didn't want to talk to him and I have been wanting to see you."

"Well, I'm glad I came too, then."

"Will you be staying in town overnight? Tomorrow is Sunday, you know. Would you like to take me to church?"

"I'd thought maybe I might."

"And you'll take supper with us tonight, after we're closed here? I know Mother won't mind."

It was his turn to look skeptical. "I hope you're right about that. I don't think she was any more happy with me than Garst was, for showing up just now."

June smiled a bit wistfully. "No, I imagine not. But she won't make you unwelcome, Gil. You should know that. She never has before, has she?"

"No, she hasn't," he admitted thoughtfully. "And it is hard for me to turn a good supper down. The cooking out at my place darn well lacks a woman's touch, that much is for sure. . . ." He let this statement trail off as he suddenly realized what the girl must be thinking: *There might never be a woman's touch out there if he never got around to asking one to marry him. There might never!*

Problem was, he wouldn't ask until he had his place on its feet, until he himself was on his feet enough to provide properly for a wife and maybe kids. A matter of foolish pride, perhaps . . . but that's the way it was. What made it even worse was the fact that, although they had known each other for over three years now, hesitation in the one still effected uncertainty in the other: Just as she could never be sure if he finally would ask, he could not be certain that she would say yes if at last he did ask. It was that way.

An awkward moment passed before June decided to turn the conversation to what seemed a safer vein. "How are things at the ranch, Gil? Are they looking up a little now?"

He shook his head. "If you call a ranch with half a barn and corrals, a cabin for a house, and almost no cattle 'looking up,' I guess they are, yeah."

"You've lost still more cattle overwinter, Gil? *More?*"

"I never had enough to matter much, June. A seed herd, that's what I called it. Two bulls and about fifty cows. It's going on three years now, and I'm down to one bull, maybe twenty cows, half a dozen two-year-olds, what yearlings are left from last year, and this year's few calves. The seed's just not sprouting much, I'm afraid. Not much at all."

June frowned. "What's happened to your cattle? I know Garst is always complaining of bears, of Old Tuffy. Did the bears get so many?"

"Garst exaggerates a lot," he said, trying not to sound unfair. "But, yeah, bears got some, lions got maybe one or two. Others froze or starved to death overwinter, and a few just plain got lost. Maybe I'll find the lost ones sooner or later, maybe I won't. Main thing is, I need a bigger seed herd, one made up of those new English breeds—Herefords, Shorthorns—which are a lot better suited to this country anyway. And I want to raise hay for winter feed so I can keep them alive. But it takes money to buy cattle and seed and haying equipment, and I just don't have enough right now. Someday I finally will, I suppose; it's just that I hate like the devil having to work in a sawmill to get it, having to wait the time it takes. That's the bad part."

"How much time, Gil?" the girl asked in a meaningful tone. "How long will it take?—going at it that way."

He shook his head. "I don't know. Maybe three more years, maybe forever, who knows. . . . Why?"

She looked away, toward the front window of the restaurant. "Three more years. It just seems so long. Isn't there some other way? I mean, does it have to be like this? So much waiting?"

Gil hesitated. These were sweetly dangerous questions she asked, ones she normally would have avoided altogether. He was not at all sure how to react to them.

Finally he said, "Believe me, it's not by choice, June. It's just that I don't know any other way—"

"But if you had the money to buy more cattle, the equipment you need, things would be different. . . . Wouldn't they?"

"Well, yes . . . I guess so. If I had enough money, by fall I could be set up pretty well, I think."

"How much is enough?"

"Oh, I don't know. Fifteen hundred, maybe two thousand dollars. Depends on a number of things. I'd like to buy cattle while cow prices are still down, because the longer I take to buy the more likely prices are to go up on me in the meantime. Two or three years from now"—he shrugged—"well, who knows. . . ."

She looked disappointed. "By then what now costs two thousand could become three. Is that what you're saying?"

He nodded unhappily.

"And what looks now like maybe three years to raise the money might turn into four, five, or even more. Is that right, too?"

Again he was about to nod yes, to confirm what was becoming a sadder truth the more they thought about it, when suddenly the front door opened and two men he had never seen before, and a third who was completely familiar, stepped inside.

The first two were dressed in gray tweed suits and funny, little tweed caps the likes of which Gil had seen only once or twice in his life. The third man was Bud Sampson, who stepped around the other two somewhat tentatively.

"Gil," he said, "I want you to meet these two fellows. Sir Robert Gatlin and Sir Henry Greenstreet—the Englishmen I was telling you about." Then hurriedly, he added, "Now, Gil, I really think you oughta listen to the proposition they've got for you. Really I do!"

Gil couldn't think of a polite way to say he wasn't interested before anyone had so much as made the proposal, so he somewhat reluctantly allowed himself to be ushered over to a table across the room, then sat quietly curious as June was enlisted to bring some coffee for the two Americans and to brew a pot of tea—if she could find some—for the two Englishmen.

He could not deny that the two foreigners were an interesting pair. Sir Robert Gatlin was a tall, slender fellow of about forty, blond with crisp blue eyes, clean-shaven, and with a sharp nose and chin. He was the "ninth baronet" of something or other, and that plainly seemed to mean he was important. Sir Henry Greenstreet, who according to Sampson was also a "titled gentleman," was short and squarish, perhaps no more than thirty-five, blue-eyed, and wore a bushy mustache that curled upward at the ends. He smoked a curve-stemmed pipe with a huge bowl crammed full of a foul-burning tobacco Gil could have done without, and his teeth were yellowed from its apparent heavy use. His mouth seemed set in an almost permanent smile and his eyes were constantly a-twinkle.

Sir Robert, the apparent spokesman of the two, looked Gil directly in the eye as he spoke. "I perceive Mr. Sampson has already told you something of the fix we are in here. He has also warned me that you may not be interested in what I am about to propose. Nevertheless, I am in hopes that you will at least hear me out. Will you?"

Gil was initially a little put off by the man's manner, but he tried not to let this show. "I'll listen," he said.

The Englishman nodded. "Good. Jolly good." He glanced at Sir Henry, then back at Gil. "It's this great grizzly bear of yours that we're after, of course. I first heard of what a grand prize he could be from some friends of mine in New York about a year ago. Two of those friends are members of my party here today, another is journalist Stuart Gladney, whose stories about the beast I am sure you are familiar with." He paused as Gil nodded, then went on. "It was Gladney who put us on to this Dawson Riddle chap, whom I immediately corresponded with and who I suppose Mr. Sampson has also told you was to be our guide on a hunt for the bear. Little did we know, however, that Mr. Riddle was not to be relied upon. I will not go into the shabby details of what happened when we arrived today, but suffice it to say that we have forever parted company with Mr. Riddle and have no intention of reconsidering the action. Unhappily, on the other hand, the circumstances have left us a bit adrift as to our plans."

Gil smiled at the understatement. "Exactly what are your plans,

Sir Robert? Of course you want to hunt the bear. I understand that. But I also understand that you have women with your party. Surely you don't plan on taking them on such a hunt. I mean, it's bad enough with three inexperienced men. . . ."

The Englishman stiffened slightly. "Sir, I am hardly an inexperienced hunter. I have hunted all over the world, as a matter of fact. In Africa for water buffalo, lion, and elephant; for tiger in India; for moose and caribou in Alaska—to mention only the more exotic of my hunts. And my friends and my wife, although less experienced than I, are certainly not neophytes. They, too, have hunted, they can shoot, and I dare say none of them—including the women—are afraid of any bit of hardship to be found in the process."

Gil wagged his head. Again the understatement: *Any bit of hardship!* He said, "But you've never hunted grizzlies before. You've probably never even seen one. . . . Am I right?"

Sir Robert remained slightly stiff. "I admit that, sir. It is my reason for being here, after all. And it isn't as if I never hunted bear. I have killed black bear in Europe many times—"

"We have black bears aplenty here, Sir Robert," Bud Sampson put in quickly, before Gil could. "But they're a mighty different breed than grizzlies. Not the same to hunt at all. . . ."

Before anyone else could say anything, June arrived with the tea, and both Gil and Bud watched with intrigue as the two Englishmen asked for and then poured small measures of milk into their cups along with the tea. June smiled, then disappeared back inside the kitchen.

Sir Robert returned to the conversation almost as if they had never been interrupted. "I may not have come in contact with these grizzly bears myself, Mr. Whitney and Mr. Sampson, but over the past year I have read endlessly about them. I am quite aware that they can be ferociously dangerous, and I know of the many feats attributed to your Old Tuffy. He is a splendid animal, no doubt, and a trophy my friends and I would give almost anything to be able to claim. That is why I want to ask what I am about to ask of you, Mr. Whitney."

Gil bestowed on Bud Sampson a somewhat less than approving glance, then said, "Go ahead. I'm still listening."

"First, as you already know, we need a guide. We must have someone who is intimately familiar with the area the bear is known to inhabit. Mr. Sampson has told me that you have a ranch in the vicinity and that you fit the bill quite well on that score."

He paused somewhat expectantly, and Gil said, "I suppose I know the mountains around my place pretty well, all right. But that doesn't mean—"

The Englishman held up a hand. "I know, I know. But please, there's more. You see, we came here knowing this hunt might not take just a day or a week. We're prepared to stay the summer, if necessary. What supplies and equipment we couldn't bring we have already purchased in Durango—or at least have attempted to. We have everything from wagons to tents to cooking utensils, and anything we still need we are prepared to buy here. We came expecting to set up a more or less permanent base camp from which to conduct the hunt. The problem is, Mr. Dawson Riddle was supposed to have established a location for this prior to our arrival—which is just one more thing he failed to do, I'm afraid. Consequently, we not only are without a guide, we are without a place for our camp."

Gil eyed him suspiciously. "And how do I fit into that?"

"Oh, that's quite simple," the Englishman said. "From what Mr. Sampson has told us it seems your ranch could hardly be a more ideal spot from which to conduct the hunt. That, coupled with your knowledge of the area, makes for an almost perfect situation, from our point of view."

Gil gave Bud another dark look, but did not say anything.

"You would, of course, be more than adequately compensated, old chap," Sir Henry piped in for the first time. "Jolly well so, I would say."

"He's right," Sir Robert said. "We've already talked about it. The same offer we made that Riddle bloke, only better. A thousand dollars outright for your services, five hundred for the use of your property, and one hundred percent of the bear's bounty money if we bring him in—which I understand is a substantial sum in its own right. Now, doesn't that sound fair?"

"More than fair," Gil had to admit. "Except for one thing.

There's almost no chance you'll get the bear. Too many good hunters have tried and failed, and there's no way I can promise to bring him to you, or even to get you a good look at him."

"Oh, come now, old chap!" Sir Henry protested. "Surely the beast can't be as difficult as that!"

"He has been for as long as I can remember," Gil maintained stubbornly.

"We ask no guarantees," Sir Robert said. "Only your services."

Gil wagged his head. "I don't know. I've got my ranch to run, and only a sixty-five-year-old hired hand to help me. We could spend the whole summer hunting that bear, and a lot of work I'd planned to get done could go wanting—"

"A thousand then . . . for the use of your property. That's two thousand guaranteed, even if we do not get the bear. Surely that will compensate you well enough."

Gil was back to looking at Bud, only this time at a complete loss as to what to say. He'd said it wouldn't take long to say no, but somehow he was finding it more difficult than that. Certainly he had no more desire to spend the summer nursemaiding this group of foreigners on a bear hunt than he'd ever had. But his conversation with June still weighed heavily on his mind, and the immediate prospect of two thousand dollars—including not having to work in a sawmill to earn any of it—was a good deal more attractive than he had thought it would be. He just could not help but consider the offer.

"I told you you'd oughta listen," Bud Sampson said. "Didn't I now?"

June suddenly reentered from the kitchen, and Sir Robert said, "Before you decide, Whitney, come outside and meet the rest of our party. I think you'll see we're not the worst of sorts at all. By Jove, you might even like us!"

Gil relented only after insisting that June go with them to meet the other hunters.

3

The part of town in which the restaurant was located lay atop a high bluff overlooking the river. Across and just up the street, Main Street widened appreciably before making a sharp dogleg back to the west. It was in this wide spot, toward bluff's edge, that the hunting party's wagons, surreys, and buckboard had now been pulled. A shade of sorts had been fashioned, using a tarp and some tent poles, alongside one of the wagons. Half a dozen chairs had been produced from somewhere, and here lounged the rest of the party, shielding themselves—or attempting to—from the afternoon sun. Six others could also be seen relaxing nearby, and to Gil, as he approached, these men looked like locals even though he knew none of them personally. According to Sir Robert, they were out-of-work miners hired in Durango to drive the wagons and surreys until the hunting camp was reached.

Somewhat pointedly, however, the Englishman ignored the drivers as he led the group up to the makeshift shade.

"Here, here, everyone!" he said brightly. "I want you to meet someone. Elizabeth, Laura, this is Mr. Gil Whitney. Mr. Whitney meet Lady Gatlin and Lady Greenstreet. And over here are our two American friends from New York—Mr. Anson Leggitt and Miss Jessica St. John. Anson, Jessica, say hello to Mr. Whitney."

Anson Leggitt, a rather stiff young man of about Gil's age, rose slowly and extended a hand. His somewhat clipped "happy-tomeetcha" seemed almost glib and his grip was less than firm. The two English ladies, both rather pale brunettes who looked amazingly like sisters, smiled faintly and nodded. Only the American girl showed real enthusiasm, and this was with a stunning smile that was only fitting of the altogether stunning personage she was.

She had light red hair, strikingly gray-green eyes, clear, milky-white skin, and a virtually flawless figure. She was tall for a girl, perhaps a year or so past twenty, and her beauty was such that in some ways even June paled beside her.

"So the savior of our expedition has arrived at last!" she said happily. "Are you normally a guide, Mr. Whitney? Are you a native here?"

Gil shook his head. "No, miss, I've never guided anyone in my life. And I guess I'm not really a native here, either. I was born and raised on the other side of the mountains, to the east of here, over near Trinidad. My mother died when I was young and my father died six years ago in a train accident. I've been here just short of five years."

The girl glanced at Sir Robert, then back at Gil. "I see. Well, I suppose you have qualifications or we wouldn't be asking you. You *have* decided yes, haven't you? I mean, we do have our problem all solved now, don't we, Robert?"

Gil looked at the Englishman, taking note of the girl's familiarity of address. Apparently Miss St. John did not feel obligated by the formality of *Sir* Robert any more than Gil imagined the man's wife or closest lifelong friend might.

Sir Robert said, "Mr. Whitney has agreed to consider our offer, Jessica. He has not quite said yes, however." He exchanged quick glances with the jaunty little Henry Greenstreet. "We, uh, were hoping you and the others might be of a bit of help in convincing him."

The girl smiled knowingly at the implication, but Gil noticed quickly that Anson Leggitt only grew more stiff. He wondered what, if any, claim the young man had on the girl.

She said to Gil, "Haven't Robert and Henry offered you enough money, Mr. Whitney? I'm sure they're prepared to be more than reasonable."

"They've been reasonable enough, Miss St. John," Gil said coolly. "That part's no problem. It's just that there are a number of complications . . . some of which I'm not sure I can deal with."

"Such as?"

"Well, first of all, a grizzly bear is no neat and tidy customer to hunt. He lives in and prefers rugged country, as far away from the sites man favors as he can get. Your friends have indicated they want to set up camp on my ranch. That's fine, but to hunt Old Tuffy we're going to have to spend days at a time away from the ranch. It may take all summer. It'll require substantial supplies and someone to keep up the camp. We'll need saddle horses, packhorses, gear, someone to cook—both at the ranch and in the field on the hunt." He looked around. "I don't know what you have in mind for those wagons and things, but most of it can't even go beyond the ranch—"

"We hadn't planned on taking the wagons beyond the main camp, Mr. Whitney," Sir Robert said. "It's just that we have brought along quite a mess of things, much of it supplies anticipated as needed for the hunt, some of it, er, of course, things the ladies will need for their comfort. I'm sure you can appreciate that."

Gil nodded. "Yes, I can. But that brings up a point I tried to make earlier. A bear hunt is no place for ladies, Sir Robert. I'm sorry, but that, as far as I am concerned, is the main problem with this expedition—the ladies."

Jessica St. John's eyebrows arched instantly. "And why is that, Mr. Whitney? You don't think we 'ladies' can fare for ourselves out here in your rugged Western wilds?"

"I wouldn't make an estimate of that one way or the other, miss," Gil replied in level though careful tones. "You very well may. Women have before and still do, of course. But a grizzly bear is a dangerous animal, and unlike other bears, it doesn't always wait to be provoked. Simply participating in a hunt where one might be encountered can be asking for a brand of trouble I'd certainly never want to put a lady through. And my understanding is that you do intend to hunt. Am I wrong about that?"

The girl shook her head. "No, you're not wrong—at least not in my case. And of course your concern is very gallant. I'm sure Lady Gatlin and Lady Greenstreet appreciate that fact as much as I do. But I'm certain, too, that we'll not present the problem you think we will. We have no intention of endangering ourselves any more than you would have us be endangered—"

It was Lady Gatlin who spoke then. "What she means, Mr. Whitney, is that neither Lady Greenstreet nor myself have any desire whatsoever to actually go on the hunt. That is why the main camp is so important. It is where we will probably be throughout." She looked at her husband, perhaps not too happily. "Isn't that right, dear?"

Sir Robert gave a slight squirm. "It's all been discussed, Mr. Whitney. The wives came to see America and this great Wild West of yours. They prefer lighter hunts altogether and will not insist on going after bear, so to speak. All we ask is that they have reasonable comfort in the process. We wouldn't dream of endangering them. Not at all."

Gil looked steadily from one of them to the other, then at the American girl. "But you . . . still *you* intend to hunt."

She smiled. "I do, yes. I love to hunt. I have my own rifle, I can ride a horse, if that's necessary, and I have been out West before, so I did not come just to see the scenery. And, Mr. Whitney, I can take care of myself. This is not my first hunt and the grizzly bear is not the first dangerous animal I have hunted. I know how to be careful, I carry my rifle as much for my own protection as to hunt, and I can stand the rigors. Truly, I can."

Gil decided he should know a good time to back off when he saw one. He looked at Anson Leggitt. "And you, Mr. Leggitt—are you a hunter?"

The young man still seemed somewhat haughty as he answered, "As it happens, sir, I am not. I consider the whole idea somewhat barbaric, as a matter of fact. I am here strictly to accompany Miss St. John. I hope you understand that."

Gil wasn't sure why the man felt the need to add that last, but he let it slide just the same. He looked at June. "Buck is going to hate me if I take this on. I know he will."

Buck Blaine, Gil's only "hired hand" and his father's lifelong friend and companion prior to the elder Whitney's death, would indeed snarl and cuss a bit at the thought of such a summer on the ranch. He was like a second father to Gil; the ranch was as much his dream as it was Gil's. He wouldn't take kindly to any such disruption of its affairs as this thing promised to bring about.

But then there was the money and what that could do for the ranch, how much more quickly the dream might be realized . . .

Gil was wavering. He knew June could see it; he suspected everyone else could too. But he didn't say anything else, and for quite a long moment neither did the girl. She knew—she had to know—that she was his main reason for even considering it. He could wait for the money, otherwise; he could work in the sawmills, and he might be satisfied to let his cow herd build more slowly, if it were just him and the old man. But he did not want to wait that long for June. She *had* to know that.

Very quietly, she said, "It's your decision, Gil. I won't cause you to regret it, either way. Believe me, I won't."

At first this didn't help him make up his mind at all; but then he realized the implied promise in what she'd said, and suddenly three years and maybe more seemed an eternity.

He turned to Sir Robert. "I don't have enough horses and gear for your needs. I can't furnish a great deal besides myself and my place. You'll need a few additional saddle horses and pack animals, and you'll need saddles and gear. And as I said before, you'll probably want to hire a cook, someone to do camp chores for the ladies. . . ."

Sir Robert's eyes lit up and he smiled his broadest smile yet. "By Jove, lad, there's no problem in any of that! Just make us a list and direct us to where to buy and hire. Whatever it takes is fine with us, right, group?"

Heads nodded, some enthusiastically, a couple only politely, and Gil said, "Another thing. If I'm to be your guide, you have to let me have the final say about things in the field. I won't do it any other way."

"Absolutely. I see no problem in that whatsoever." The Englishman put his hand out. "Is it a bargain, then, Mr. Whitney? If so, I believe it will be a bloody good one for all of us. Indeed I do!"

Gil took his hand. "I hope so. I sure do hope so," he said, and then turned a second later to a beaming Bud Sampson and added so only that individual could hear, "You better hope so, too, Bud. Damned if you hadn't!"

What he hadn't counted on at all, a few moments after that, was June pulling him aside and saying, "Take me on the hunt, too, Gil. Please."

"*What?*"

"You heard me. Ma's got other help at the cafe and I know I can convince her to let me." Then, as he gawked at her speechlessly: "I'll be the camp cook, do the chores, even wait on the ladies if I have to. *Anything.*"

Still, he was incredulous. He had no idea what to say.

"You're doing this mostly because of me, aren't you?" she went on, seemingly a little embarrassed but determined nevertheless. "Well . . . *aren't* you?"

"You know I am."

"Then I just want to help out. I know my way around a camp, and certainly you don't have enough help as it is. You know Buck isn't going to want to leave the ranch work entirely for something like this. Oh, please, Gil—don't say no! Please!"

"Well . . ." He was trying desperately to think, but this had come too fast for him. How *could* he say no? "Well, maybe . . . if your mother agrees. . . ."

Her eyes lit up. "Oh, Gil! Thank you, Gil! You won't regret it, believe me!" Then she paused to cast a look over at Jessica St. John, who was now standing several yards away, beyond earshot. "Besides"—she smiled a little self-consciously—"how can I let you spend the summer alone around someone who looks like her? How can I now!"

4

June was a strong-willed girl. Even Mrs. Greer was unable to say no to her. The proposed experience with the hunting party was such a novelty that it was also a real opportunity—the kind not just everyone would get a chance to have. After all, what other contact was June ever going to have with such a sophisticated and interesting group of people as these? How could even a very protective, somewhat disapproving mother say no to a daughter who realized this perhaps more than anyone else?

"You know I don't like it," the woman told Gil, off to one side that evening after supper. "But June is almost twenty. It'll do no good for me to interfere. You just make sure nothing happens to her that we'll both regret. Do I make myself clear?"

The double meaning of this was all too evident to Gil, who replied, "Yes, ma'am. I understand."

Mrs. Greer's expression softened momentarily. "Well, I know I shouldn't be hard on you. I trust June, and I guess I trust you, too. Just please watch after her, will you?"

"Like a hawk, ma'am," Gil said, glad to get off that easily. "I promise."

Later, as he was preparing to leave, he made one last effort to dissuade the girl. "There's no telling what I've got us into here, June. It may be a real disaster. Are you sure you won't reconsider?"

She smiled. "Not a chance. And I know you can handle it, Gil. Have faith in yourself. Why, you may even get the bear. Wouldn't that be something!"

Nevertheless, he went to his room at the hotel beset by second thoughts and doubts. He had never organized anything like this before; he had no idea how many complications might yet arise, nor how he would handle them if and when they did. He did not sleep well. He rolled and tossed about as one thing then another occurred to him as having to be done before the hunt could even be started. He awoke the next morning all but convinced he should back out. Fact was, he went downstairs and over to Mrs. Greer's restaurant for breakfast determined to do just that the minute he saw the first representative of the hunting party.

As luck would have it, he met Sir Robert coming from upstreet just as he arrived at the restaurant. Gil knew where the Englishman had been. A block or two back, where the bluff lessened considerably, a side road led to the river. A large flat area along one bank had been found where the wagons could be parked for the night and the stock pastured. The drivers had pitched camp nearby while the hunting party had put themselves up in the hotel. Sir Robert had obviously just finished an early-morning check on things below.

"What a bloody good morning it is, eh, Whitney?" The Englishman positively beamed at him. "You have no idea how relieved I am to have our problem of yesterday solved. I don't know what we would have done if you hadn't come along."

Gil just sort of nodded, what he had been wanting to say somehow jamming in his throat.

"I take it you're on your way for a bite of breakfast," the

Englishman went on. "What say I join you? Give us a chance to list some of those blooming supplies and things we need to buy. How about it?"

"Well, I have to take Miss Greer to church in a little while, but I did want to talk to you," Gil said lamely, knowing already that he was not going to be saying what he had wanted to at all. "It is going to take some planning, all right. I guess now is as good a time as any to get at it."

An hour later they emerged from the restaurant, a somewhat sobered Sir Robert holding in one hand a surprisingly long written list of things they would need. But he wasn't discouraged. Many of the things he had bought in Durango, although somewhat extravagant, were needed (tents, bedding, heavy-duty clothing), and he seemed determined to proceed no matter what the cost of the additional items. Gil, on the other hand, had decided that he himself might just as well become equally determined to see the expedition through, no matter how great the distraction of its party. He had contracted to provide them a place from which to base their operations and to furnish them himself as a guide—and that was what he was going to have to do.

But Lord, what a mess it could turn out to be!

Well, they simply had to start someplace and see how it went from there. First, the things on the list: Saddle horses and pack animals (Gil knew a place or two to get animals that were sufficiently gentle to do the job), then saddles and gear (no problem, as long as you had the money), food staples and a few more cooking utensils (easy enough, but a significant portion of the list), lanterns, coal oil, additional ammunition for rifles (the party had more than enough weaponry, proving that they had anticipated thoroughly along these lines already), and sundry items too numerous to recall aside from the list.

It would take a day or two to get it all together, and Gil was already considering sending someone to the ranch to explain ahead of time to Buck what was about to happen. He hesitated to do this, for he doubted that the old man would believe it without seeing it for himself, anyway. But he hated to spring it on the old guy without warning. After all, the last Buck knew, Gil had simply gone into town for a few small supplies, the mail, and to see

June. He wouldn't be looking for anything like this to descend on him, and Gil at least owed him the forewarning. Someone would have to be hired and sent straightaway, Sir Robert offering quickly to pay whatever it cost.

Aside from this and the purchases that needed to be made, the prospect of getting everything to the ranch was the next problem. There was room enough in the wagons for the extra gear and supplies. That did not present a problem. But how to get the wagons there did. No one in the party seemed to know how to drive one and Gil doubted that any one of them would stoop to it if he did. The drivers from Durango could be retained for that purpose, but then what to do with them after that? Sir Robert, it turned out, had anticipated the problem. Although the wagons and surreys had been purchased outright, the buckboard had only been rented, and that in one of the driver's names. He and his fellows could return to Durango in it, and when there turn it in at the livery stable and pay for its rent with money given them by Sir Robert. All very neat and efficient.

The next problem would be getting the newly acquired saddle horses and packhorses to the ranch. Gil would see to that by simply tying them to the wagons and letting them trail along behind. The hunting party could be distributed among the two surreys and the buckboard just as they had been on the trip from Durango. Gil would ride his own horse and June would ride with one of the women. It would not be a fast-traveling circus; a good half a day would be required for them to make the trip. But the roads were mostly dry now, and, barring breakdowns, they should arrive in good shape once they were actually under way.

So the plans were formed. Everything began to seem set. Gil, Sir Robert, and Sir Henry would be busy getting things together throughout the next couple of days. The women would use the time to mostly lounge around the hotel and rest, with the exception of June—now the official camp cook—who had some getting ready of her own to do. The American, Anson Leggitt, seemed strangely disinterested, and although he promised to be of little help, he at least did not seem inclined to get in the way. By the third day all should be ready for the trip to the ranch.

So there it was: Perhaps the strangest "expedition" ever to

come to San Juan country was preparing to get under way. A certain ripple of excitement began passing through not only the participants who prepared for the experience but the townsfolk who looked on in growing wonderment as well. Even Gil found himself caught up in the atmosphere, although he was not sure he felt encouraged by the thought that what they might encounter could just as easily be failure as success. But this fact hardly seemed to bother the hunters. Sir Robert exhibited nothing but confidence. Sir Henry proved even more the eternal bubbling optimist. The two English ladies appeared reserved but quietly anticipatory. Jessica St. John bestowed a rather spirited "Let's get on with it!" on the group. Only Anson Leggitt remained less than enthusiastic, and his somewhat aloof demeanor was simply beyond Gil to figure out or, at present, even to worry about.

One way or another, nearly everyone who looked on had a view about the expedition, ranging all the way from hilarity to curiosity to quiet amazement. Nevertheless, Bud Sampson summed it up for most by saying, "I don't care what happens with the bear, this hunt is gonna be something—I mean, really *something!*"

Off to the side, the two Ute Indians who had looked on in amusement that first day watched over the next two days without expression. They could be forgiven for doubting that this particular group of hunters would ever so much as set eyes on the one they called Spirit Bear.

CHAPTER 2

THE EARLY EFFORT

1

Six years earlier, local ardor for trying to bring in the bear was at a fever pitch, perhaps at its peak. It was early summer and the bear had been credited with killing a number of cattle belonging to a particular ranch located fifteen or so miles south and slightly east of the basin. A well-known hunter from across the line in New Mexico, a man named Jones, was contacted to see what he could do. This Jones had, at the time, what was considered one of the best packs of lion and bear dogs in the country. It was thought that if anyone could run the big grizzly down, Jones and his pack of hounds could.

Jones arrived at the ranch with his dogs two days after he had been sent for, confident that only a matter of time would be required before the big grizzly marauder was brought to bay. Straightaway a hunt was organized. Jones and his dogs—accompanied by the rancher and half a dozen cowboys armed and fully primed for the hunt—were taken to the site of the most recently discovered kill. The dogs sniffed and rushed around in great excitement, then formed a pack as one dog then the rest took to the trail, howling happily as they went. The eight horsemen tore along desperately behind them, hopeful that soon the big bear would be in their sights. The dogs were quickly well out in front and after only a few minutes could be followed with any speed only by the sound of their constant baying.

Two hours later the horsemen came upon them, yowling

joyously up at a small pine tree. High in the tree was a small black bear that apparently must have wandered onto the trail somewhere along the way and had diverted the dogs from the big grizzly's scent. With too much of the day gone to reestablish the original trail, the hunters were so disappointed they left the black bear in the tree and returned directly to the ranch.

A week later, after two more such incidents with black bears, a hot trail was discovered about midmorning one day near a fresh deer kill, around which huge grizzly tracks, made sometime that morning, were plentiful. Once again the dogs took off in great ecstasy and the hunters strung out behind, working to keep up as best they could.

For over two hours the hunters followed the distant baying of the pack, falling farther behind all the while. Then, after a bit, the howling seemed no longer to be outdistancing them and its tone was noticeably changed. They were led up into unbelievably rough country. The baying of the dogs grew louder, and the hunters' hearts leaped. The hounds clearly had something cornered. The riders pushed their horses hard as they drew ever closer and strange yelps began to accompany the howls of the dogs. Something was very definitely going on up there!

Then, suddenly, after only a brief spell of gradual diminishment, the baying and yelping stopped. The dogs could no longer be heard. The hunters drew up in consternation. Presently they located the dogs' tracks and continued on. It took about forty-five minutes, but they finally found the pack—or what was left of it—in a small clearing at the base of a vertical rock bluff where the bear must have at last been brought to bay. There had been seven dogs altogether when the hunters had last seen them. Four were found dead within ten yards of one another, horribly torn apart by sharp, long claws. Two more were found whimpering pitiably nearby, badly mangled and near death. The seventh must have escaped or crawled off in the brush to die, for it was nowhere to be found at all.

And there was no bear. Only those same huge paw prints they had seen earlier, imprinted here and there and all around where the dogs had fought their valiant, bloody struggle to hold their quarry until the hunters arrived.

The hunters, this time, returned to the ranch in complete dejection. The bear was gone and there would be no tracking him now. Bright and early the following morning, the man Jones headed back to New Mexico, vowing never again to put good dogs on the trail of so vicious a monster-beast as this particular grizzly must have been.

Gil had heard the story a dozen times, and he told it to the group during the trip to the ranch. They had pulled up to rest the horses where the road turned east at Echo Canyon, and were presently lounging on blankets spread beneath a tall, well-branched pine while the wagon drivers checked the teams' traces.

"Wouldn't be much interested in hunting with dogs myself," Sir Henry observed after a moment. "Doesn't seem very sporting to me. What do you think, chaps?" He looked around, although mostly at Sir Robert. The women had all listened attentively and with varying degrees of horror at the outcome—but none of them could be expected to have an opinion on how sporting the nature of the hunt might or might not have been. Plainly, Anson Leggitt didn't see fit to class the effort as sporting no matter how it was done. Only Sir Robert, and perhaps Gil, could be expected to see the point.

"Ordinarily, it's the best way to get a grizzly," Gil said pragmatically, "aside maybe from traps."

"I suppose they've bloody well tried those too, eh, Whitney?"

"They have."

"And with no more success than the dogs, I take it." Sir Henry grinned knowingly through his mustache. "Certainly not, if the bloody beast is still running around loose. There must be a hundred stories of how you folks have tried and failed to get him. A hundred and more."

Gil shrugged and Sir Robert said, "Of course there are. That's why we're here. The challenge of it all. The very fact that the blooming animal has eluded death for so long already is what'll make it so bloody fantastic when we pull it off. Nobody else has been able to!"

"If you pull it off, Robert," Lady Gatlin reminded patiently, her pale, aristocratic bearing masking what Gil had come to believe was a fully spirited being underneath. "I think Mr. Whitney's point is just that, you know. That all these good men have tried before is good reason why you shouldn't be disappointed if you fail also."

"And, too, you fellows," Lady Greenstreet put in, "he's making a point about the danger involved. A bloody bad beast, this bear— isn't that so, Mr. Whitney?"

Gil smiled. His first impression that the two women were sisters had been correct, Lady Greenstreet being the younger by two years, but hardly to be outdone otherwise. "Yes, ma'am. That was one of my points, all right. Any grizzly can be bad business; this one is doubly bad."

"Now, come on, Whitney," Sir Henry said good-naturedly but with a couched warning just evident within his tone. "Let's not be scaring the ladies. We've got our rifles and there'll be no fewer than three of us out there. Even the worst grizzly bear should be no match for that."

"Right-o!" Sir Robert exclaimed, rising. "You've hit the mark on that one, Henry. And I'm getting anxious to be on with it. How far to the ranch, Whitney?"

Gil sighed and also got to his feet. "Three miles, Sir Robert. Three miles up the canyon from here."

To call it a "canyon" at this point was almost a misnomer. It ran generally from northeast to southwest and was, where the road entered it, a grassy, mile-wide valley bounded on either side by parallel-running, pine-timbered ridges. Down the valley floor, beneath a long, thin line of willows that from a distance was its only visible demarcation, a tiny creek trickled serenely. Here and there, cattle—a few of them Gil's, hopefully—grazed peacefully. There were no people other than themselves, no ranches, in sight, and the road was little more than a set of infrequently used wheel ruts meandering along the footslopes of the north ridge.

But the road was essentially dry and only in a few places did the ascent of the valley cause them to encounter more than a gradual grade; and the very fact that Gil had been careful not to attempt to bring a wagon out when the ground was wet overwinter made it less rutted and much more easily traveled now. They made decent time throughout and in only one or two spots had any trouble at all.

The valley narrowed as they went, but if anything became even more beautiful. There appeared to have been a little logging on the ridge to the north of them, and now and then a few cows were encountered, but otherwise the area seemed almost pristine. They were in the last half mile before Gil's ranch came into view.

The first surrey rounded a curve just after noon, and there it sat, tucked prettily against a hillside to one side of a beautiful grassy meadow with a willow-lined creek cutting down its center: The half-finished barn and corrals, a horse pasture, the cabin, and about half a mile above this a picture-like grove of towering cottonwoods where seemingly the meadows terminated and a true canyon took over.

"Oh, how pleasant!" Jessica St. John burst out the moment she saw it. "But how isolated, too! Do you really live way out here, Mr. Whitney? In the winter, too?"

"I'm afraid I do," Gil said, pulling up alongside the surrey, the back seat of which Miss St. John shared with June, while the front was occupied by one of the Durango drivers and Anson Leggitt. "But it's not as far from town as coming by road will make you think. Horseback, there are shortcuts a man can take. And anyway, I sort of like it here—isolation and all."

"I should hope so!" the girl exclaimed. "What do you think of it, June? Have you been here before?"

"No," the Western girl said in somewhat reserved tones. "I've . . . never had a proper opportunity to come before. But yes, I do like it. It is very beautiful."

At the barn and corrals—a good hundred yards short of the house—they pulled up to leave the extra saddle horses and packhorses that Gil and Sir Robert had purchased in town. This done, they proceeded on up the road.

At the house, a beautiful English setter, colored white with black spots and ticks, came bounding out to meet them.

"I say, Whitney," Sir Robert exclaimed. "You have good taste in dogs. What's his name?"

"We call him Fleck," Gil said, dismounting and looking toward the house. "Hey, Buck! You here?"

He had added onto the original three-room cabin "Texas style," which in effect created two cabins under one roof with a breezeway in between capable of housing or passing at least one wagon through. Out back was a woodshed and outhouse and up the hill a ways a chicken coop was under construction. A year ago Buck had planted cottonwood cuttings all around the front yard and all but one had survived and were growing rapidly. They were thinking of putting up a picket fence as soon as a few higher-priority items like the barn and corrals were completed.

Gil motioned for those on surreys and wagons to also get down. "Hey, Buck! I know you're around because the dog is. Come on out, will you?"

A familiar figure suddenly materialized coming from behind the left cabin, bowlegged and wizened, leathery-faced with a three-day-old gray beard and a few unruly locks of white hair showing beneath a broad-brimmed black Stetson that was but one of several of the old cowhand's trademarks. He stopped and for several moments took in the strange sight before him.

"Well," he finally said in a sort of crackling drawl that was also a trademark, "I reckon I didn't believe that kid you sent out here. I thought sure someone was playin' a joke on the old man again."

"It's no joke, Buck," Gil told him. "I want you to meet these people. Sir Robert and Lady Gatlin, Sir Henry and Lady Greenstreet, Miss Jessica St. John, and Mr. Anson Leggitt. You know June, of course. My friends, this is Buck Blaine. Those other fellows over there are drivers Sir Robert hired in Durango. They'll be going back after the wagons are parked and the teams unhitched."

The old man stared at the group, then swung his gaze back to Gil. "Where?" he asked brusquely.

"Where? Where what?"

"Where you gonna park them wagons, that's what. Look around, boy—tell me where."

Gil looked. Aside from the meadows, level places where wagons could be parked and tents set up were at something of a premium. The hill behind the house and along the road to the barn was brushy and in places steep. Gil himself owned only one wagon, and it was down at the barn. It had not occurred to him that there might be a problem parking the hunting party's wagons and surreys. And really, there were places up the hill from the house that, although not ideal, would serve—he knew there were. . . .

Then he realized what it was that actually concerned Buck. It was the people, not the wagons. Where was he going to put the people?

Well, there was a suitable location for that too—a spot that was not only close by but was reasonably level, with shade and about a hundred and fifty feet from the main house—the very spot where Gil and Buck proposed to one day build a bunkhouse. Not a bad location at all for the camp—except maybe from Buck's point of view, which would likely prove this or anywhere on the ranch too close for his comfort.

Well, later they would talk about that. Just now, Gil knew he had to be firm. He turned to Sir Robert and his group. "We'll unload the wagons right over there, then park them on up the hill a ways. If your drivers are willing to help out, they're welcome to stay the night and head back tomorrow. It'll be a big job, I know, but you've tents to set up and dozens of other things we've got to decide where to put until they're needed." He turned to the women. "You ladies can use the cabin as a place to rest up. Just give Buck and me a chance to clean things up a bit first and it'll be all yours." He glanced at Buck meaningfully.

The older man gave him a baleful look but didn't say anything. The others seemed lost in their appraisal of what apparently was to be their campsite and the job at hand. It was hard not to notice at least one or two mild scowls.

After a moment, Gil added, "Look, for a place that is both near the house and near water, this is about the best I can do. If it's not suitable . . ."

Sir Robert quickly raised a staying hand. "Don't worry, please! It's not that at all. Fact is, it's a bloody good spot, eh, group?" He looked around at the others, then added, "Well, we said we would take the rough with the easy, didn't we?"

It was Lady Greenstreet who gazed longingly up the canyon and said, "I dare say that beautiful grove of big trees would be a prettier site. Of course, if it's important that we be close to the house here . . ."

Gil smiled inwardly. "You're welcome to look the grove over," he said. "It's alongside the creek and it is pretty up there. I just assumed you ladies would rather be near here when the men are off on the hunt and you're left alone. That way, you're less likely to find a bear in camp with you, not to mention skunks, coyotes, badgers, porcupines, lions. . . ."

He didn't need to say any more; Lady Greenstreet immediately turned to her husband. "He's not fooling me, is he, dear? Those animals might really come right into a camp?"

Sir Henry smiled. "Bloody well they might, woman! Those and more, from what I've heard."

Sir Robert said, also smiling, "I think your campsite will do fine, Mr. Whitney. Come on, everyone, what say we get something to eat and then pitch in to put things in order? Fair enough?"

No one objected this time. They had packed lunches before leaving town, and the women headed directly for their lunch baskets as the men began trudging toward the nearest shade.

For a few moments, Gil and Buck simply looked on. "Well," the older man finally drawled, "you've really let yourself in for something this time. Damned if you haven't."

Gil looked at him. "Wait till you hear what they're paying me, Buck. Wait till you hear that before you judge."

The old man's eyes were flinty blue and were especially piercing as he replied, "I'll be interested in knowin' about that, all right. Yes, I will. But mark my words: No matter how much it is they're payin' you, you're sure as hell gonna earn it. Takes no more'n one look to figure that out. One look!"

2

Gil never doubted that the old man was right in what he had said. *How* right, he was destined to spend the next few days learning.

The first project was laying out the campsite. For the more permanent base camp, the party had purchased four relatively large tents, each with room enough for two people to sleep comfortably within. When first the tents were unloaded, however, it seemed there were canvas and tent poles everywhere and nothing made much sense to Sir Robert and his group as to how to set any of it up. Finally Gil and Buck figured out the pattern of things for them, and with help from a couple of the wagon drivers soon had the four tents erected.

A sort of semicircular arrangement being decided upon for their placement, the center two tents were then designated for the married couples and the one on the side nearest the house set aside for June and Jessica. Anson Leggitt would have the fourth and farthest tent all to himself.

While this was going on, the wagons were being further unloaded, and when empty were then taken one at a time up the hill to be parked. The teams were unhitched, taken to the barn for a light graining, then turned loose in the horse pasture. For the time being, most of the supplies and gear not immediately needed were stacked in the breezeway between the two cabins of the main house. Innumerable other items were stored inside the tents, leaving both Gil and Buck amazed at the volume of things the party had brought along.

"Did you see how many trunk loads of clothes they brought?" Buck asked from off to one side as the last wagon was being unloaded. "Enough to suit out half a regiment, at least!"

Gil smiled. "I don't think most army regiments would go for the kind of uniforms they'd find in those trunks, Buck. Ladies' dresses and things mostly, I'd guess."

The old man wagged his head. "Lord, what in the world they gonna need fancy dresses around here for?"

"Only He may know," Gil said, still smiling.

Next morning the wagon drivers rolled up their bedrolls, hitched two horses to the buckboard, and piled aboard. One of them told Gil as they prepared to pull out on their way home, "Can't say this was the worst job I ever had, but I don't envy you yours. In some ways I'd like to hang around just to see how it turns out . . . but I don't think I will. Ha! Ha! See you, Whitney!"

Gil watched them ride off and almost wished he could go with them.

The balance of the day was spent organizing both things and people. A camp routine had to be established; and although it was plain that the individual members of the party were more accustomed to having things done for them than doing for themselves, it was soon found that they could show plenty of pluck where pluck was needed. Camp chores were discussed and to some extent divided up among the campers, with June gladly taking the lead both as cook and chief "chore boy." Sir Robert was so appreciative of her contribution he offered to pay her a salary as camp cook. She declined acceptance, saying the experience alone was worth the work. And besides, she was helping Gil out mostly. If anyone should pay her, he should!

On this good-natured note, one thing that occurred to Gil was how much easier it would be if all the cooking were done inside the house. It just seemed silly any other way, the camp being right there on the kitchen doorstep as it was. Consequently, he even offered one section of the cabin to the women to sleep in.

"Sleeping in tents is going to grow tiresome plenty quick, if you ask me," he told them. "I'm sure Buck and I can work things out to make one side available to you. Three rooms altogether, if you want them."

He was rejected unanimously. The two married women, quite understandably, preferred to stay with their husbands. Jessica St. John said no, she had come expecting to sleep in a tent and in a tent it would be. June, who probably knew best what Gil was warning them about, demurred probably for no other reason than she wasn't about to be the only one who did otherwise.

Thus a compromise was reached. The section of the cabin containing the cookstove would be set aside primarily as a cookshack and dining area for the entire group. It would be fully available to the hunting party. Gil and Buck would make their quarters the opposite side of the breezeway and would simply share the cookshack with the others.

June, in particular, appreciated the arrangement. Not only were the cooking chores going to be greatly simplified—and more in line with a woman's culinary talents—by having a stove rather than a campfire to cook over, but she knew how chilly mountain air could become of a morning, even during June and July. The warmth of the cookstove would certainly make breakfast a more pleasant experience for everyone; and because each section of the cabin had its own fireplace, drying both soaked bodies and clothing after a sudden summer downpour would at least be possible if they could just get inside.

So a regimen began to be established. By the third day, some of the initial excitement over sleeping out of doors had worn off, but by the fourth day, the members of the hunting party were so settled into the routine they had established that Sir Robert was becoming anxious to get on with the bear hunt.

"I say, Whitney, let's do some planning here," he told Gil that evening as supper was being prepared. "How do we go about approaching the bear's territory? What'll be the details? Packhorses and camping out away from the ranch, I presume."

Gil smiled. He and Buck had taken advantage of the past few days to do some work on the corrals and barn and they had been hoping for at least two or three more days before any move toward the hunt was initiated. It didn't look as if it was going to work out that way, but Gil wasn't surprised and consequently was not disappointed.

"Something like that, yeah," he said. "There's a lot of country to cover and the bear could be almost anywhere. It's going to be a problem knowing where to start."

"How much country, would you guess?"

"Well, I don't know. Grizzlies have greater range than black bears. Some say fifty miles or more, some say less. My guess is Old Tuffy'll range as far as any of them—in a season's time. This time of year though, I'd say somewhere mostly east and south of here is our best bet. Figure ten, maybe fifteen miles for a starter—probably someplace in the vicinity of old Squaretop over there."

The Englishman's eyes followed Gil's. They were looking almost due east. "So that's the name of that funny, flat-topped mountain we've been seeing. Or did you tell me its name before? Well, never mind about that. What makes you think the bear will be in that neighborhood?"

"There's a basin south of there where some say he makes his winter den. The Blanco River runs through the basin, and what we call the Little Blanco, one of its tributaries, drains this side of

Squaretop. My nearest neighbor claims he's lost calves to bears already this year, and he claims Tuffy's tracks were found around one or more kills between here and Squaretop. I'd say in that vicinity and maybe toward the basin where the Blanco runs is where we should look first."

Sir Robert could not seem to take his eyes off the mountain, which from this view looked like some gigantic, carelessly carved square head made of pure rock.

"It certainly looks to be rough country from here," he commented appreciatively. "And there's still snow up there. Is that normal for this time of year?"

Gil nodded. "Pretty normal. It's over eleven thousand feet in elevation up there, nearly twelve. Some of the mountains beyond go over thirteen, and it's not unusual to see snow at those heights as late as mid-July."

"And that's the bear's territory, eh?" The Englishman scratched his chin thoughtfully, marveling.

Again Gil nodded. "The rougher the better is the way I suppose a grizzly looks at it. You'll find that out soon enough, I'm afraid."

Sir Robert eyed him appraisingly. "You seem to know the animal quite well, Whitney. I'm beginning to think you undersold yourself when we first talked to you, I really am."

This time Gil shrugged. "I admit I've spent some time trailing around behind that old bear you're after, Sir Robert. And I've spent a good deal of time talking to old-timers who live around these parts about him. But I don't want to operate under false pretenses. I'm a stockman, not a bear hunter or a guide. It just seems important to me that you're aware of that. . . ."

They were standing in back of the cabin, still looking east as he spoke, and Sir Robert seemed about to make a reply when they heard the dog, Fleck, barking out front. They turned just as Buck appeared in the breezeway behind them.

"Gil, we got company out front. I reckon they wanta see you."

Gil eyed him quizzically. "Who is it?"

The old man spat and said, "Well, it's Garst Cunningham, for one. I reckon it's who he's got with him you won't believe."

Gil frowned. "Tell me anyway."

"Well, it's none other than that no-account Dawson Riddle.

Would you believe that? Garst Cunningham and Dawson Riddle!"

3

The two men had dismounted their horses and were lounging in front of the cabin. Their eyes were cast in some amusement on the half circle of tents a short distance away. They had with them, in addition to their mounts, two packhorses, each carrying what looked to be a full pack.

"Well, Whitney, I didn't believe it when they told me, but now I guess I've got no choice," Garst Cunningham observed flatly. "You really have hooked yourself up with these pilgrims. Damned if you haven't!"

Gil looked toward the camp. Sir Henry and the two English ladies sat in the shade near one of the tents. The jaunty little Englishman was dressed in a light shirt with pants tucked inside knee-high boots, and he wore a funny-looking little sun helmet, which Gil presumed he and Sir Robert—who had one just like it— had picked up somewhere in Africa. The women wore long dresses, casual for them perhaps but oddly regal-looking for their surroundings, and they lounged in so genteel a manner that one almost expected servant boys to come scurrying about at any moment. As to the other members of the party, Jessica St. John had just disappeared inside her tent and Anson Leggitt was nowhere to be seen. June was inside the cabin, cooking supper.

Sir Robert gave Cunningham a hard look, but spoke to Gil. "I don't believe I've had the pleasure, Whitney. I take it you know this gentleman?" His inflection on the word "gentleman" was decidedly sarcastic.

Gil sighed. "Sir Robert, this is my neighbor from just over the hill—Mr. Garst Cunningham. You already know Dawson Riddle. . . ."

Riddle, a dark, dumpy, almost slovenly sort who hadn't shaved in a week and probably couldn't remember when he had last bathed, straightened slightly and grunted something unintelligible. Sir Robert ignored him completely.

Cunningham said, "Howdy, Sir Robert. Didn't mean to offend you. Just teasing my old pal Whitney here. How about it, Gil—when you going out after the bear?"

Gil gave him a noncommittal shrug. "We were just talking about that, and I reckon it'll be soon. Why? What are you and Dawson up to?"

Cunningham's smile was a very thin one, almost a smirk. "Well, Dawson and me just recently learned we had something in common, you see. That's right. Dawson lost a job he'd sure been counting on—which you know about, of course—and is now out of work and needing an income. And me, I'm still having fits with Old Tuffy. Just yesterday, in fact, some of my boys came across another kill, this time a fat two-year-old steer. Me and Dawson, now, we'd both like to get the bear—him for the bounty money, me to cut down on losses. So we're teaming up. I'm taking Dawson up the canyon now, to show him where the boys last saw the bear's sign. It's not far from here, no more'n three miles up. The old reprobate was headed south when they lost his tracks yesterday."

Gil simply stared at him. This was hard to believe. Garst Cunningham teaming up with Dawson Riddle!

"And you just had to ride through here to get there, right?"

"Well, we didn't just *have* to," Cunningham admitted. "Could've gone to it from my place, I guess. But it's your range as much as anybody's up there, so I just figured coming by to let you know was the neighborly thing to do."

Gil turned to Riddle. "And you, Dawson? You're going after the bear anyway, even though you know these people are here to hunt him?"

"It's a free country, ain't it?" Riddle grumped, perhaps a little too quickly. "He's anybody's bear till he's brung in, ain't he?"

Sir Robert still stood at Gil's shoulder, and being nobody's fool, instantly seethed. "Mr. Riddle, if you are in any way addressing your actions to your recent misadventure with me and my party here . . . well, sir, just *say* so!"

Riddle glowered at him. "I'm goin' bear huntin', Englishman. I ain't addressin' you or your party one way or another. Fact is, you can all go hang for all I care."

Sir Robert almost had to be restrained physically by Buck and Gil to keep him from charging the man.

"Sir . . . by God, sir! You are a lout and a beggar. I demand that you apologize! I demand it!"

"Whoa, now! Just hold on!" Buck interjected quickly, trying to calm the man down. "You don't have to pay his kind no mind, Sir Robert. And you, Dawson. You got no call to be crusty. These people are guests here and so are you."

Buck's tone carried with it a good deal of authority, which Dawson Riddle knew the older man could back up. The would-be hunter-guide continued to glower but wisely kept his silence. Sir Robert, struggling for control now, turned to Gil and Buck.

"I'm sorry, Whitney, Buck. I should not have spoke up in the first place. If these men have any business here, it's obviously not with me. I think it would be best if I excuse myself completely."

Gil felt this should not have been necessary, but for the good of the situation he let him go anyway. As the Englishman disappeared inside the cabin where June was fixing supper, Gil turned back to Cunningham.

"Anything else, Garst?"

The other man's eyes were on the cabin. "I hear June is here. Is that true?" His tone was less jovial than before, and there was a definite dark undercurrent in his demeanor.

"Yes, it's true. She asked to come. Why?"

Cunningham shrugged. "Just wondered . . . no reason, I guess." He looked as if he wanted to say something else, but had decided against it. "Mostly, I just wanted you to know I'm putting Dawson on the bear's trail, and that it don't matter to me who gets the bastard, so long as someone does. Hope you understand."

Yeah, Gil thought, *I understand*. But he only said, "Well, that's good of you, Garst. Thanks for coming by."

Cunningham took one more look at the cabin. Gil didn't know if the man suspected June was there, but he did suspect that the girl was making it a point, once again, not to show herself in Cunningham's presence. The rancher straightened and said to his companion, "Come on, Dawson. Best be on our way if we don't want it to go dark on us before we make the trail. See you, Whitney. Buck."

"Yeah, see you," Gil said, doing his best to maintain the civility of the moment.

Only Dawson Riddle broke it. The two men had remounted their horses and had gathered up the lead ropes of their pack animals when Riddle edged his horse up close to where Gil stood.

He said, "Cunningham's bein' nice about it, Whitney. Nicer'n he feels, let me tell you. That's his business. As for me, I just figure I got somethin' to prove to that smart-mouthed Englishman, and to you too. I'm gonna get that bear out from under you. By God, I am!"

"You got yourself fired, Dawson," Gil reminded him calmly. "You were already out of the picture when I came along."

Riddle stared back at him, revealing little and choosing not to retort. He reined his horse around and said to Cunningham, "I'm ready if you are."

The two men rode on up the canyon, more or less on a course that would skirt the upper meadows and the cottonwood grove, and only Garst Cunningham looked back as they went. His look was not a friendly one, and it was this that upset Gil much more than did anything Dawson Riddle had done or said.

"Well," Buck said slowly. "What do you think of that?"

Gil shrugged. "I'm not sure. I guess Garst is put out because June's here but couldn't bring himself to say so. Dawson's mad because he lost his job. They're bent on taking it out on me, and the way to do that is to bring the bear in before we can. It's both stupid and foolish, but I figure that's about what there is to it."

Buck wagged his head skeptically. "Well, at least they came by to tell you first."

"Yeah," Gil said, remembering distinctly Cunningham's parting look. "Yeah."

4

Despite assurances from both Gil and Buck that Dawson Riddle posed little real threat to the bear, the episode with the ex-guide only served to make Sir Robert more anxious than ever to get on with the hunt. And since, after all, that was what this whole business was about, Gil felt compelled to oblige him the soonest way possible.

They spent all the following day getting ready—organizing gear, food supplies, figuring out which saddle horses were gentlest, how many pack animals to take and how much grain would be needed for the horses, and of course outlining the general territory they would try to cover.

Gil and June talked about it that evening after supper. It was almost sundown and they had decided to take a walk down to the barn—practically their first opportunity to be alone together since the hunting party had arrived at the ranch.

"I'm hoping to hold this first time out to no longer than about a week," he told her as they walked. "It's pretty futile really—a crew like this hoping to come across the bear without dogs or anything else to aid them. I've told Sir Robert that a dozen times but he's come to try and try he intends to do. He's a stubborn one, I'll say that for him."

"But you do know the bear has been in the area. Didn't Garst claim he was going to show Dawson Riddle where they had last located fresh tracks?"

"Yes, and I'm sure Garst knew what he was talking about. We'll try to find those tracks, of course. But the trail won't likely be fresh now, and better hunters than we are have tried following him over better trails than we'll likely find. It's just a place to start, that's all."

They drew up at the corrals, the smell of freshly peeled pine poles strong in the air. A few more days' work and they would be finished with much of the basic layout. It was beginning to look like a real ranch now. Even the barn was beginning to look like a barn. Buck still had a lot of the finishing touches to put on the outside, but inside, six horse stalls with feed bunks, a saddle shed, a hayloft, a milking parlor with stanchions, and a calf pen were almost completed—with only the stanchions still to be installed and that being the case only because they still did not have a milch cow.

June leaned against the corral fence, staring between poles at eight to ten horses corralled inside, ready for an early saddling next morning. A lane fenced with barbed wire gave them access to the creek for water, and they had been grained less than an hour before supper.

The girl frowned slightly. "And you really are going to let Jessica go along? You've decided that for certain?"

"I don't see that I have a choice," he said somewhat painfully. "She seems determined to at least go out on this first 'bit of a jaunt,' as Sir Henry calls it."

June looked up at him. "I wish I could go."

He gave her what really was a pained look this time. "And have your mother kill us both, in case the bear doesn't? Come on, June —don't add to my troubles, please."

She smiled wistfully. "Oh, don't worry. I won't. It's just that it'll be so boring around here while you're gone. And—and Jessica . . . well, she won't have a proper chaperone. I mean, she is a woman going alone into the hills with four men—and an unmarried woman at that!"

Gil stared at her for a moment, decided she was mostly kidding, then sighed. "Look, that's her problem. And besides, she's got good old Anson tagging along to guard her reputation. Certainly Sir Robert or Sir Henry or I aren't any threat to her honor. . . ." He eyed her a bit anxiously. "You believe that, don't you?"

"Oh, Gil." She almost laughed. "Of course I do. I know, too, that Jessica can take care of herself, and she's forever and a ton away from home anyway, so who's to know what she does? And for some reason, in her case, it just doesn't seem so out of the ordinary a thing to do. I mean, Jessica is different from the kind of girl we're used to. I can't explain it exactly, but she's just so, well, so much more her own person, so much less charged by convention. Do you know what I mean?"

Slowly he nodded. "I think so. Sort of like she can go on a bear hunt—or anything else that strikes her fancy—anytime she chooses. Right?"

June smiled softly. "Yes, that's right. And everybody here knows it. Except maybe Anson. . . . Did you know they had a terrible argument over it last night?"

"No . . . no, I didn't," Gil said, surprised. He had spent about an hour the past evening talking with Sir Robert and Sir Henry, then had turned in for the night. He had paid the hunting party very little attention otherwise. "Did you hear them argue?"

She shook her head. "No, I didn't hear them. Jessica told me about it when she came to bed. They had gone for a walk, sort of like us tonight. I guess Anson waited till they were out of earshot before he said anything to her about it."

"He doesn't want her to go on the hunt?"

June laughed. "Hardly."

"Well, I suppose I can understand that. If she was my girl, I doubt if I would either."

"Yes, but for different reasons, I hope," she said flatly.

He looked at her quizzically. "I guess I don't follow you."

"Well, I may be unfair to him in thinking this, and I'm sure he really is concerned about Jessica's welfare—both her safety and her reputation—but I think he feels as much as anything that if she didn't go then he wouldn't feel called upon to either. He considers this whole affair an uncivilized bore, but apparently he's been trying to get Jessica to marry him for over two years and he's bent right now on not letting her out of his sight until she says yes. Personally, I wonder if he's not wasting his time. Jessica may someday marry, but it's awfully hard for me to believe she might pick someone as unlike herself as Anson Leggitt."

"Why did she let him come along then?" Gil wondered aloud.

"I don't know. Maybe she didn't have any say in the matter, since I believe it was Sir Robert who invited him in the first place. Anyway, that's something I guess I just didn't think to ask her."

Gil wagged his head. "And to think I've got to take both of them along tomorrow. Heaven help me!"

Again June laughed. "Well, at least you've already warned them who's going to be boss on the hunt. That should help some, shouldn't it?"

"Sometimes I wonder," he said, looking a bit less than confident.

She turned and put a sympathetic hand on his arm. "Let's talk about something else for a while, okay? Tell me things about the ranch. You said you wanted to grow hay. Where? How?"

He smiled. This was a subject he could warm to easily and she knew it. He motioned to an area beyond the barn that extended well to its either side. "Right out there—the meadows," he said. "I'd like to introduce new grasses—timothy and redtop, possibly— to go with the native bromes and such. I'd like to cut ditches on some kind of contour so I can irrigate—I think that can be done, you know, even if we have to go all the way to the Little Blanco to get the water and build several miles of ditch to get it here. I figure I've got seventy-five acres, maybe more, I could irrigate. I could raise enough hay to winter several hundred head of cows on that, June. Several hundred at least. . . ."

5

They were awakened at gray dawn by the gobbling of wild tur- keys and the scolding of magpies. Gil helped June get breakfast started, wolfed down his own, then headed down to the corrals to begin the saddling of the horses. An hour later Sir Robert, Sir Henry, Anson Leggitt, and Jessica—all decked out in sun helmets and riding clothes—presented themselves at the corrals. Buck, June, and Lady Gatlin and Lady Greenstreet strolled down a few minutes later to see the hunters off.

"I say, these western saddles are a load, aren't they?" Sir Henry observed speculatively as he appraised both his mount and its gear. "Aren't those blasted stirrups a mite long, Whitney?"

"We'll see when you're mounted, Sir Henry," Gil told him. But even after this was accomplished and Gil had adjusted them to what he considered the proper length, the Englishman still looked askance at the setup.

"By Jove, you've probably never seen an English riding saddle, have you? Well, I guess I'll just have to adjust. Are you sure this beast can carry all of this and me too?"

"He'll carry it," Gil assured him, less concerned about that problem than whether or not Sir Henry could stay aboard in the event the animal decided to buck. He'd had everyone lead his or her mount around a bit to make sure the humps came out of the horses' morning-cold backs before allowing anyone to mount, but that didn't guarantee a thing, he knew.

As it turned out, only Gil's own horse even made the attempt to pitch, and this inclination was quickly ridden out of it before they left the corrals.

They had three packhorses to lead and Gil assigned the two gentlest ones to the two Englishmen. He also rechecked all of the saddle girths, rifle scabbards, bedrolls, and packs before they left. He had marveled before at the weaponry the party carried with them—the finest high-powered rifles Europe had ever manufactured, with beautifully hand-carved stocks and at least one, Sir Robert's, having been inlaid with gold, silver, and ivory. Gil's own Winchester Centennial Model, .50-95 Express—although a rifle he was otherwise quite proud to own—seemingly paled in comparison. Still he took comfort in knowing that, in the area of firepower, at least, they were as prepared for grizzly as any group of hunters had ever been. He only hoped they didn't fall down completely in too many other areas.

They rode out amid waves and "good-byes" and "take cares," holding first to the edge of the upper meadow, then passing beneath the tall cottonwoods and heading on up the canyon, the dog, Fleck, trotting easily along behind.

Before long they came upon day-and-a-half-old tracks of shod horses and knew they were following the route taken by Garst Cunningham and Dawson Riddle. They followed the tracks for about two miles before coming upon a spot where the two men must have camped for the night. Just past this, they found where Cunningham and Riddle must have the next day begun some trailing of their own. The hunting party took to this new sign eagerly.

Along about midmorning Gil found the single, fairly well preserved paw print of a very large bear. It was in the mud of a creek bank, could not have been less than four or five days old, and was the only such track not obliterated already by the tracks of other animals or the two horsemen and their pack animals who had preceded Gil and his group. Nevertheless, the print was distinct. It was a right front, and it had three toes missing. The big white-and-black setter sniffed curiously at the trail, but apparently found the scent too old to be exciting.

"Do you think that's our bear?" Sir Robert asked after a keen examination of his own. He was plainly impressed by the size of the print.

"Well, the track is big enough, and the missing toes match. I'd like to see a left front, though. He has two toes gone from there, and if we found one of those to go with this one, we'd have almost certain confirmation."

"How do you know that? I mean, how was it determined that such a track belongs to this particular bear?"

Gil smiled. "Every now and then someone actually sees Old Tuffy—more often than not some poor sheepherder who gets the wits scared out of him over the experience and loses a lamb or two to boot. But in any event, he's hard to mistake when you see him and people have had plenty of occasion to go directly to his tracks afterward. He's had those same toes missing for a number of years now, and the fact has been confirmed many times."

"What caused it? The missing toes, that is."

"Steel traps, I reckon—back before he got too smart to stick his foot in one. He probably chewed the toes off to get loose. That or they just fell off after he'd dragged the trap and whatever clog was attached to it around for a few days. Either way has the same effect, of course."

"How awful!" Jessica St. John exclaimed from nearby. "He would really do that? Chew his own toes off?"

"Sure, he would—to get loose. Chew a whole foot off if he had to. It's not so unusual."

"Barbaric," Anson Leggitt said. "Utterly barbaric, such traps."

"Yeah," Gil said, but let it go at that.

They followed the horse tracks for nearly a mile without finding even a portion of another paw print, and finally came upon a place where it seemed obvious that the other hunters had also lost the trail and had given up. Numerous game and livestock trails crisscrossed here and there, and lacking further tracks it was impossible to tell which path the bear might have taken.

"Not much we can do," Gil told them along about noon. "He was headed south and east, that's all we know. I figure Garst went on home and left Dawson to go it alone from here. He'll be guessing just like we will from now on."

"But he has a head start on us," Sir Robert worried.

"Doesn't matter. The bear could be anywhere. Without dogs or a really fresh trail to work from, we're all depending heavily on luck at this point. Dawson's got no advantage, other than he's only one man and can probably move around with less fuss and bother."

The Englishman frowned. "You think our numbers could hurt us?"

"They could, yeah."

They spent the balance of the day riding higher and higher into ever-thickening timber—tall pines, dense aspen thickets, spruce, and fir. They crossed the Little Blanco, gurgling delightfully with fresh snowmelt from higher up yet, and turned slightly more to the south. To their left now, old Squaretop—always their best landmark—loomed impressively. Now and then a small patch of snow could be seen lingering on a north slope beneath thick stands of trees where sun's rays seldom reached. Deer and elk were encountered on several occasions and caused to go slipping quickly away among the trees and brush. A badger grumpily stood his ground in the middle of the trail, forcing them to go around and making Gil have to call Fleck away lest the dog bite off more than he could chew. A pair of porcupines were seen straddling limbs high overhead in adjacent pine trees. Magpies and jays scolded constantly from above. And finally, a beaver dam turned a tiny creek into a six-foot-deep pond right where the trail should have crossed, causing them to have to forge a new route through an unbelievably thick growth of aspen.

They climbed higher, turned more and more to the south, and a good two hours before sundown struck a satisfactory site for a camp. It was located along the edge of a beautiful, small meadow that was enclosed on all sides by thick timber, had a small creek running down its center, and provided plenty of graze for the horses.

The hunters were perfectly glad to stop when they did. Jessica had more than adequately proven her claim that she was not a bad rider, but she was also one who had adamantly refused to ride a sidesaddle. Now she had to be helped from her horse, complaining of a soreness she had never known or expected to know before. The two Englishmen and Anson Leggitt managed to dismount on their own, but did not appear to be any less affected by the long day's ride than the girl.

"I'm rubbed so raw I don't think I'll ever be able to get back on that thing," Jessica proclaimed unashamedly as Gil unsaddled her horse for her. "I never dreamed what a real horseback ride might be like!"

"And if you were smart," Anson Leggitt said from nearby, "you'd not have set out to learn."

She shot him a look but did not say anything. Gil said, "Well, nothing says we have to go at it this hard tomorrow. We've made it into some pretty good bear country now. We can go a little slower from here on—unless we find something, of course."

"And then we go rushing pell-mell, is that it?" the girl asked.

He smiled. "Depends on what we find. But I wouldn't worry too much; we're likely to do a lot more looking than finding just now. It shouldn't require a lot of rushing 'pell-mell,' as you call it."

Not just the girl cast him a relieved glance at this pronouncement.

Anson Leggitt wandered down to the creek and disappeared in a willow patch while the rest of the party busied themselves with the camp. Gil showed Sir Robert and Sir Henry how to unsaddle and hobble their horses, then unloaded the packs. Bedding (canvas-covered bedrolls for the men, a bedroll and a small, one-person tent for the girl) was stripped from their saddles and packs, a fire pit built, wood gathered and a fire started, both coffee and hot water for tea put on to boil, and cooking utensils—Dutch oven and skillet, primarily—produced. It wasn't the most organized camp Gil had ever pitched but his fellow campers were willing both to learn and to help, and he suspected things would go smoother as time went along. Anson Leggitt even pitched in to help Jessica carry the dishes down to the creek for a washing after supper. It was about all he did, but he at least did that.

"He's a bloody strange bloke, all right," Sir Robert told Gil as they watched the two young Americans go. "Rich as sin and unused to doing a blooming thing he doesn't want to do, you know. His father's fortune, it is. Of course, I'm one to talk, but I think there is a difference. At least I have interests, such as my hunting and traveling. Old Anson doesn't know what he's missing, really."

"He does seem to have one interest," Gil said, indicating the girl.

The Englishman wagged his head. "Only reason he's along, of course. Out of his head to have her, he is. Couldn't care less about this trip otherwise, sad to say."

"Why'd you let him come along then?"

"His father wanted him to come . . . and the old chap is a rather special friend of mine, I must say. He felt it might do the boy some good to go out on a real adventure, that sort of thing. I just couldn't turn him down. You know how it is."

It was Gil's turn to wag his head. "Well, I wish you could at least get him to carry a rifle. He may not want to hunt, but who knows when he might need something for his own protection. I know I sure don't feel comfortable up here without a gun; nobody I know does. Maybe not a lot can happen, but there are things."

At first the Englishman laughed and said, "Like grizzly bears running loose, eh? Ha! Ha!" But then his expression changed, as if something had just occurred to him. He leaned forward almost as if he didn't want Sir Henry—presently cleaning his rifle just across camp from them—to hear. "That brings something up I've been wanting to ask for some while now. We, er, saw some of those American Indians of yours on the road from Durango and some more in town the day we met you. Now admittedly they didn't dress much the way I expected them to—more like white men, I'd say—and Jessica assures me they're all confined to some sort of nearby reserve or something, but those I saw didn't look very confined. Are they . . . I mean"—he seemed somewhat embarrassed—"do *they* represent a possible danger up here? I've heard and read a lot about your bloody Indian wars and so on. Is that what you're talking about?"

Gil confined himself to a grin, despite the almost overwhelming urge to laugh outright. "No, Sir Robert, I don't think so. Not anymore. Oh, sure, there's a little trouble now and then over on the reservation, but no uprisings or anything like that. The Utes— that's what those Indians you saw were—surrendered themselves to the army years ago. Those things you've read about are pretty much in the past now. Very much so, in fact."

"But those we saw . . . they certainly weren't on the reservation, were they? How are they allowed to run loose like that?"

Again Gil smiled. The man really was concerned about this. "They can be given permits to leave—so they can work at the sawmills, or on ranches nearby, or sometimes just to hunt and fish off the reservation. They are great hunters, the Utes . . . at least they used to be. Nowadays, they have them growing corn and herding sheep."

"Do they hunt grizzlies?"

"I suppose they used to, maybe not much anymore. Actually, I think the grizzly represents some sort of religious significance to them. I'm not sure to what extent, but I do know one of their main ceremonials is the Bear Dance, held each March to celebrate the end of the hibernation season. It's also supposed to be a courtship ceremony. Nowadays, it interferes with corn planting and other spring work, so there are those trying to get them to move the date back to May or June. Who knows, someday they may even forget why they do it, just like they may no longer have the big bears to hunt or revere."

"By Jove, that last strikes me as sort of sad," Sir Robert said. "Do you really think the big bears—the grizzlies—will someday all be gone?"

Gil shrugged. "I imagine that's one of those far-reaching questions someone like me isn't supposed to be able to answer, Sir Robert. But I'm not sure that man and the grizzly will ever find a way to coexist. Each is too pugnacious when it comes to sharing a territory. And there aren't that many Old Tuffys left to forever outsmart us. The average grizzly is a tough customer, but he isn't nearly as impossible to bring in as Tuffy has been. Not by a long shot."

This seemed to make Sir Robert even more thoughtful. "But you stockmen, you all want him dead. He kills your cattle and sheep and must be brought to earth for it. Isn't that why all the rewards on his head and all the effort to get him?"

For a long moment Gil just looked at him. It seemed about all that could be said about it, and yet was so utterly, utterly simple.

Too simple. Strange, he thought, how this way of thinking had never bothered him before.

But all he said was, "That about sums it up, I guess. I guess it just about does."

6

It was both a short week and a long week, or so it seemed. Short because by its end they had accomplished nothing tangible in respect to locating the bear; long because seven days and six nights out simply seemed that way. Certainly, the experience was such that they were all more than ready to head for home by its end.

Not to say it was an empty time, for that wasn't so at all. Despite moving the camp only twice after that first day, they covered a lot of country and saw plenty before they were done. They saw perhaps half a dozen cinnamon or black bears, deer and elk every evening and every morning, and on the third day Jessica was given the opportunity to shoot her first mule deer, for camp meat. It was a fine young buck, which she brought down with a single bullet placed cleanly through the heart, thus seeming to prove that she really was as good a shot as she had said she was and that she was *not* necessarily a liability to have along.

Even Anson Leggitt wasn't a total loss. He wasn't much help around the camp or with the horses; he suffered far more than anyone else from the rigors of the riding all day and sleeping on the ground all night; and he cared least among the hunters for the hunt and all that went with it. But somehow he finally did become impressed with the beautiful scenery, the wildness of their surroundings, and for a while at least even ceased to complain. Once he was even heard to mumble that he was no longer sorry he had come along, although Gil surmised that this was not going to be a lasting philosophy if he had to do it again and again.

Sir Robert and Sir Henry, on the other hand, not only did not complain, they seemed to purely thrive on everything about the experience, including its inconveniences, about which they were almost completely practical in their viewpoints. It was what they

had come here for, an encounter they had craved and even more:
An adventure in which they participated fully, from camp chores
to chafed rumps and inner legs, from deer fly bites to ticks and
chiggers, from bearing their own guns to saddling their own
horses, from near encounters with skunks and porcupines to sunburns and a thorough drenching during a brief thundershower the
fourth day out. A complete adventure in every way. . . .

Except they did not find the bear. They didn't even see a grizzly. They saw fresh tracks on several occasions, tracks they
thought might be those of a grizzly. They found where a fairly
large bear had rolled aside a huge rotting log to get at the grubs
beneath it, then followed the animal's tracks down a trail that
same bear must have been using regularly. Gil even pointed out
where the bear had stepped repeatedly in its own tracks, made perhaps only the day before, as it went. It was a trait of grizzlies to
do that, he told them, but other bears might do the same, and
thus they could not be certain that it was not a large black bear
rather than a grizzly that they followed. And since they never saw
the animal, of course they were left never to know for sure.

So, aside from what they'd seen that first day out, they were unable to locate any sure sign of Old Tuffy. The bear could have
been on the move at the time and might have left the area altogether by now. Or he might not have. He could be almost anywhere. Lacking good clues, they simply had no way of knowing
where else even to look for him.

Apparently they weren't alone in this, either. Twice they came
across the fresh tracks of three horses, all shod: A mounted Dawson Riddle with two packhorses, Gil was sure. But plainly Riddle
was just wandering around now, very much the same as they were.
He, too, had failed to relocate the bear's trail. This was some con-
solation to Sir Robert, who still worried that Riddle might get to
the bear before they did, but it did nothing to encourage them re-
garding their own odds on success.

They went all the way south to the Blanco River, followed it
upstream into the basin Gil had told them about, then circled
back in the direction of the towering peak that was Squaretop,
angling toward its western slopes all the while and eventually

coming full circle almost to where they had first seen the big bear's tracks seven days earlier.

At this point, they were almost home, and late on the seventh day they rode back within sight of the ranch. They were tired almost to the point of exhaustion but were not especially discouraged, for Gil had warned them enough times about that, and already they were talking about the next trip out.

"We'll just keep at it till we find him, that's all," Sir Robert announced flatly. "We've got the summer still ahead of us, by Jove. We're bound to have some luck before it's over, eh, Whitney?"

"It makes me shudder just to think of it," Anson Leggitt was heard to say as he rode along behind. "A whole summer of this . . . Good grief!"

"Oh, don't worry so, there, Anson," Sir Henry told him. "You'll live, and you might even be the better for it. Besides, you can always lay out a hunt or two here at the ranch. You too, eh, Jessica? No use overdoing it, you know."

The girl had already indicated that the one hunt might have been more than enough for her. "It's not that it hasn't been worth it. It was an experience I'll never forget," she told Gil as she rode immediately alongside of him. "But it was sort of rigorous for a woman, and I did make you a promise about that. I think I'll probably restrict my little outings to something closer to home from now on, if you don't mind. I can see it's going to be men's work to actually bring in that bear."

They were approaching the house from the upper meadows and the three women and one man they had left behind could already be seen waiting for them out back.

"But you will take me out for a shorter ride now and then, won't you, Gil?" the girl went on. "Or maybe even a fishing trip— in between hunts, that is."

He looked at her, startled. "Why, yes, I suppose so. I imagine the other ladies might like that also. June, too. . . ."

She looked a bit disappointed at this response, but only said, "Of course. The other ladies too, I'm sure. That would be nice for us all."

The way she had said this bothered Gil somewhat, but no more was said about it as already they were nearing the house, where

June and the others proved so happy to see them again that they at first didn't even think to ask whether or not the hunters had had any success with the bear.

Which was all right with Gil. He, too, was glad to be back. He quickly forgot all about what Jessica had said and was looking forward with relish to whatever period they would spend on the ranch before going out again.

For a few days at least, he intended to avoid thoughts about the bear whenever and wherever he could.

Nine miles away, however, at the base of a rugged footslope of Squaretop Mountain, there was one individual who had no such intention. The only thing on his mind *was* the bear, and that was the way it was going to stay until he found it—in which area things were suddenly looking up.

Dawson Riddle had just located a remarkably fresh trail, and was at that very moment crouched over a set of huge paw prints, the right front of which clearly missed three toes, the left front, two.

CHAPTER 3

IN THE SHADOW
OF SQUARETOP

1

It wasn't the first time a hunter had attempted to engage the bear one on one—without dogs, without other hunters to back him up, without traps. Just hunter against the hunted, man against beast, the studied intellect of the one pitted against the wary instinct and animal cunning of the other.

A man named George Selkirk from Utah was a hunter whose ways these were.

No stranger to mountain country, Selkirk was a curious hold-over from a bygone era, a true anachronism, a mountain man still roaming trails long overgrown since the real figures of those earlier times—the Jim Bridgers and Jed Smiths—had set foot on any of them. George Selkirk was aware of this. But whatever he lacked in his timing, he made up for in mettle, a brand of which his predecessors would have been proud to acknowledge.

George Selkirk was an expert hunter, and he was obsessed with the killing of grizzly bears. He was said, in all, to have killed over forty of the beasts; and he was also said to carry claw and tooth marks from one of them over half of his body, including his scalp where a strange streak of white hair covered a bad scar. He was fifty-two years old when he came to make his effort to bring in Old Tuffy. It was late summer, the year, 1891.

Selkirk was interested in the bounty money, of course, but only mildly. He'd been hearing a lot about this bear called Old Tuffy.

More than anything else he wanted to be the man who brought in the hide of the Great Silver Bear of the San Juans.

For over a month he tramped the bear's known haunts. He found tracks matching those described to him as belonging to the famous grizzly. He found a number of kills—deer, livestock, elk. He attempted to wait in hiding near this or that half-eaten carcass, cached obviously by the killer for a return meal. But the bear was smart; somehow it must have sensed, on each occasion, that all was not right, and if it approached at all it always turned back before the hunter caught sight of it.

Undaunted, the hunter resorted to early-morning and evening stakeouts of oft-used trails and likely-looking berry patches; he tried again and again to track the animal. He had precious little success, coming close only once, one late afternoon when he thought he caught sight of the big silver-coated marauder disappearing into thick foliage straight ahead . . . but too late, for it was soon dark and the tracks were lost almost before the hunter could get well into things the next day.

And so it went. The leaves turned colors and began to fall. The hunter grew worried that the first winter storm would put an end to his endeavors for the year. The high country would be relatively impassable and the bear would make its winter den. George Selkirk might very well return to civilization empty-handed— something he very much did not wish to do. Everyone knew he had gone after the bear; he had never failed so completely before.

Finally one day he procured an old horse from a ranch lower down on the Blanco River. He led the horse back up into the mountains, to an area he knew the bear had recently hunted. In a small clearing dissected by a well-worn trail with the big bear's tracks firmly imprinted on it, he shot the horse from fifty yards away and left the carcass undisturbed. He took up hiding in nearby brush where the wind was least likely to give him away, yet from which the entire clearing could be seen. He waited all one day and into the next. Daylight waned that second day and still the carcass lay undisturbed. The bear had not shown. The hunter grew discouraged, but he told himself he would wait at least till midmorning the following day.

There was a gleaming full moon that night. It rose after dark and flooded the clearing with bright moonlight. Along about nine o'clock, the hunter had all but fallen asleep. But then something happened—something he could not immediately identify brought him alert. Was it a sound? Something aside from the routine noises of the night? Or was it something only the sixth sense of a hunter might cause one to detect? Certainly he hadn't seen anything; his eyes had actually been closed.

He studied the clearing and its fringe carefully. A very slight breeze stirred among the dry stems and leaves of cured tall grass. A few straggler leaves tumbled lightly from a nearby stand of white-barked aspen. The body of the dead horse was a dark blotch on the center of the clearing, and the stench of decaying flesh came to him, causing his stomach momentarily to turn. But he was glad the smell came to him, nevertheless: He wanted the breeze in his face, of course.

For almost five minutes he sat there, tense and alert. Nothing happened. He relaxed slightly. Then, just as he was about to decide that his sixth sense had been playing tricks on him, movement caught his eye. A form appeared on the far side of the clearing—something big, something very big. The bear . . . it had to be the bear!

Suddenly, he realized he was gripping his rifle so tightly his fingers hurt. For the first time in a long time, he actually shook with nervous excitement. It was the bear! The animal had moved almost into the open now and was less than seventy-five yards away. Even from such a distance he could see that it was a huge bear, clearly outlined, dish-faced and hump-shouldered, as big as any George Selkirk had seen in all his years of hunting them—a grizzly beyond a doubt.

It was very cautiously studying the dead horse. Twice it rose to its full height to sniff the air, sort of swaying back and forth rhythmically for several moments before dropping back to all fours. Selkirk realized with a shock that he himself had not moved. He'd perhaps had as good a shot as he was ever going to get, and had not so much as raised his rifle!

The bear shuffled cautiously forward, its light coat seeming to shimmer in the moonlight. Slowly it approached the carcass, circled it warily, rose again on its hind feet. At last Selkirk raised his *rifle. Keenly aware that he might never get another chance, he fired . . . perhaps too quickly.*

The bear only grunted, reared momentarily higher, then dropped and whirled with startling speed toward cover. Selkirk fired twice more before the big animal crashed with a roar into the brush at clearing's edge and disappeared. The man was left staring at a vacant scene, deathly silent now, and he was shaking, if anything, even harder than before. He could have sworn that at least two of the three shots had hit home . . . but the bear hadn't even been slowed!

For perhaps ten minutes Selkirk crouched there, afraid to move, waiting, hoping the bear was either out there dying or had kept on running. Certainly there was nothing the hunter could do now except wait for daylight and then hope to trail the animal to wherever it had gone. He sat there five more minutes, and still he had not fully ceased shaking. Why was he so affected?

And then he knew. Suddenly there was a tremendous crashing in the brush behind him. Heart in his throat, he whirled and tried to come to his feet. A huge form towered over him, gleaming almost white in the moonlight. He tried to raise the rifle, but a massive paw swiped at him, catching him on the shoulder and sending the gun spinning into the air. Hoarsely he screamed as the bear was upon him. He went desperately for his knife, but even as he did so he knew he did not have a chance.

It was over quickly, but they did not find what was left of his body until the following spring. . . .

2

Dawson Riddle found where the bear had made a kill less than an hour after he'd first found the tracks. He was looking south, Squaretop towering behind him, rough country falling steadily away from him to the fore.

He could tell it had been a kill by the disturbance of the ground and brush all around, the great pool of blood and scatterings of more blood beyond that; he knew it was a deer kill by the tracks, the scattered bits of coarse hair. But the carcass was gone;

clearly the bear must have dragged it away toward some more secluded spot where it could enjoy its meal. There was no telling how far away this might be.

Still, for the hunter, the moving of the carcass was good news; it made tracking so much easier. And in the case of Old Tuffy, Dawson Riddle knew he needed all the help he could get. He knew in his heart—even if he could scarcely be brought to admit it openly—that no man alone would be a match for this great beast.

But he had committed himself; he was determined to show those Englishmen, Gil Whitney, all of them . . . determined to present them the bear they themselves so wanted to get, to hold it over them. He knew his hadn't been the best of lives so far; there had never been a lot he could be proud of. It was about time something happened to change that . . . about time.

He had basked warmly in the brief limelight brought him by that newspaperman from New York and his writings about the bear. But it had been a tarnished basking at best. The locals had considered Dawson's involvement a joke, pure sham. They had laughed at him, belittled him, dismissed him as an impostor. They did not believe the name Dawson Riddle should be mentioned in the same breath with that of the silver bear.

Well, he would just have to show them all. A fair step in that direction had been made upon his striking the rather surprising alliance with Garst Cunningham. That had told Whitney something. Now he had to get the bear. Only that accomplishment would adequately repay that Sir Robert Gatlin and his crowd for what they had done to him. Dawson Riddle *knew* he must get the bear.

And now he had his chance in front of him. Staring him starkly in the face were tracks so fresh he could smell the heavy scent of the bear yet upon them, and blood so recently spilled it had not yet fully darkened—a real chance.

But there was much pressure in knowing this. He was keenly aware that such a chance might not come again. He must not make a mistake, for even the slightest miscalculation—a noise at the wrong time, allowing himself to be seen too soon if at all, or worse, getting upwind and subjecting himself to the animal's keenest sense, its ability to smell—could ruin everything. Whatever he did, he must not let the bear know he was on its trail—not before he had it in his sights, at least. This would be difficult, for the bear was smart and knew how to slip away without being seen the moment it realized that it was being stalked. It had happened before to some very good hunters; it could easily happen again. Just thinking about this gave Dawson pause. He must carefully consider his every move.

He looked around. The afternoon shadows were growing long; sundown would come in less than an hour, full dark in well under two. He looked at the blood on the trail and reaffirmed in his mind that it could not be an hour old. The bear had not likely gone very far . . . but could he catch up to it while there was still light? Could he do it at all if he chose to play it safe and wait till the next day, letting the trail begin to grow cold in the process?

It was not an easy decision to make. The bear was unpredictable; it might gorge itself on its kill and move on; it might hang around for a second meal . . . but how was the hunter to know? Any other bear and he would assume it would hang around. But this bear did not operate like just any bear; there just was no telling what it might do.

For Dawson Riddle the risk of waiting was too great to take. He felt compelled to follow the trail now, immediately; he could not bring himself to let it grow one second colder. But he wasn't a complete fool. He would proceed very carefully and go only as far as he thought prudent. If darkness caught him still short of his quarry, of course he would stop and wait for the next light of day. It would be the best he could do, what he would have to settle for, if it happened that way . . . but somehow he really didn't think it would.

He left his horses behind. He just could not conceive of slipping up on the elusive Old Tuffy with a saddle horse and two packhorses in tow. It would be too noisy a way to go, too cumbersome; the risk of alerting the bear and blowing the whole thing was too great. On foot might be more dangerous—the hunter already felt frightfully helpless without his mount and instinctively did not like walking—but he doubted he would ever get close to the bear any other way.

The trail was not difficult to follow. Lacking any real reason to suspect it was being followed, the bear had stayed to a well-worn path. Faint blood spatterings and signs of the carcass being dragged continued to accompany the tracks, but there were no signs that the bear had been slowed much by its burden—which was not surprising. A bear of this one's size could lug a full-grown elk or a steer a mile or more if necessary; a mere deer carcass was almost no challenge at all.

Dawson had gone less than what he surmised was half a mile through an area thick with spruce, fir, and aspen when he struck a tiny clearing that the path crossed but the bear had not. On the opposite side of the clearing was a rocky hillside overgrown with oak brush; on the other three sides, tall trees all but hid the sky from the ground. The bear's tracks led to one side, plainly skirting the clearing.

It was a highly furtive movement the bear had made here, and it should have given the hunter pause. But the sun was nearly down now and Dawson Riddle could think only of how short time was growing if he wanted to find the bear today. Intently, he followed the sign as it circled the clearing and came eventually to a point on the other side where the brushy hillside began.

Here he did pause. The bear's tracks, fresher than ever now, entered the heavy brush on another well-worn trail. Quite obviously the animal knew where it was going. Dawson of course did not, and the denseness of the brush gave him a distinct chill. Much of it was too high for even a man on horseback to see over. Should he go in there he would be unable to see more than a matter of a few yards ahead much of the way. It would also be next to impossible to negotiate without making at least some noise. . . .

He glanced around indecisively. The shadows were long and dark now. It was not a good time of day for him to see well—keen vision ordinarily being the hunter's only advantage, because a bear's eyesight is extraordinarily poor. And the forest was quiet, strangely so. Sound, any sound, would carry far under such circumstances—and poor hearing was *not* one of the bear's characteristics. At the moment there was no breeze, but the hunter knew this only made it more difficult for him to tell whether he was upwind or downwind of the bear. It did not mean his scent could not be detected if and when a breeze did stir.

Very cautiously he entered the brush, feeling his way with every step now and making no sound. He knew the bear was up there someplace. There was fresh scat on the trail here, very fresh. He knew he must be as careful as at any time before in his life.

He followed the trail carefully as it angled its way uphill. Perhaps a hundred yards along he came to the first real opening in the brush, no more than fifty yards across and with but a lone, scraggly pine near its center to break his view of the other side. Heaving a cautious sigh of relief, he studied the area, then entered the opening.

The trail passed directly beneath the pine tree, and it was here that he came across the deer carcass—a full-grown doe lying crumpled at the base of the pine. With a shock he realized that the carcass had not been cached. It had not been eaten from. No attempt had been made to hide it by scratching up leaves and twigs and dirt atop it. It had been dumped, abandoned—perhaps in a hurry. . . .

His heart suddenly drumming inside his chest, Dawson Riddle backed away as if stung. He switched his gaze to his surroundings. Something had spooked the bear away from its kill. What? Jesus, he *knew* what! The bear had become aware that it was being followed, had got wind of Dawson somehow. But where was it now . . . ?

Something crashed in the brush dead ahead. Dawson jerked as if hit, then backed away instinctively, all but forgetting the rifle in his hand. Fright clutched him. The crashing came again; he remembered the rifle. Thoughtlessly he jerked it to his shoulder and fired into the brush. A sharp, coughing grunt was followed by a maddened roar. Dawson backed up again, except this time catching a heel on a tangled root and stumbling backward. His balance destroyed, he fell, right elbow striking rock solidly as he hit the ground. Only dimly did he hear the rifle clatter against rock a few feet away as numbing pain radiated throughout his arm. He rolled over, moaning and holding the elbow in acute agony.

He did not remain this way long, however. The bear suddenly burst into the open, snarling, lumbering directly for the fallen hunter. Desperately Dawson came to his feet; even more desperately he looked around for his rifle. He couldn't find it . . . and he realized there wasn't time to look further. Thinking faster than ever before in his life, he did the only other thing he could do: He turned to the scraggly pine tree. A low branch hung just within his reach, and forgetting completely about the pain in his elbow and arm he leaped for the limb, clutched it, dangled for an excruciatingly long instant, bettered his grip, then pulled and kicked with all his might to get a leg over. This done he was quickly astride the limb and reaching for the next higher branch, standing then as he heard the bear growling angrily beneath him now. Afraid to look down, he scrambled higher, knowing he must completely clear the bear's reach lest he be caught by a foot and dragged back down.

He must have been fifteen feet up before he stopped and looked back at his attacker. It was just as well. Had he looked sooner he probably would have frozen, would never have made it. The bear was on its hind feet, stretched to full height, its massive dished face and paws seemingly only a foot or so away.

Dawson Riddle clung to the trunk of his scraggly haven like a shipwrecked sailor clinging to the last floating timber of his sunken ship. He blubbered, perhaps for the first time in years, something that resembled a prayer. It *was* a prayer, one of thanks —not just for the fact that he'd made it to where he was, but that in a case like this his attacker was a grizzly bear and not a black bear, that grizzlies, unlike their normally less ferocious cousins, do not—cannot—climb trees.

But that didn't mean Dawson was completely out of danger. The bear below him was not only an extraordinary grizzly, it was plainly an enraged one. Its roar was like that of two tremendous objects being scraped together, fearsomely resonant. For a few minutes the animal slapped and swatted at the lower tree limbs in frustration; then, rearing once again to full height and placing its front paws against the trunk, it began to shake the tree. Dawson hung on like a leech, praying now that the monster below him wouldn't uproot the thing.

But strong as it was, the bear couldn't do that; the tree wasn't pretty, and it had not grown as tall as it should have for its age, but it was sturdy of trunk. The bear could not uproot it; it could not shake the trunk hard enough to dislodge a desperately tenacious Dawson. After a while the animal settled back on all fours, then its haunches. It stared up at the tree with tiny piglike eyes and grunted. Dusk had settled; the bear's silver-grizzled coat looked dark in the poor light. The beast did not look as if it would be going away soon.

Dawson Riddle continued to cling to his perch.

Presently the bear contorted itself so as to put its nose to its right haunch, sniffing, whimpering a bit, then licking the haunch almost like a cat cleaning itself. The man in the tree looked on curiously. Then he realized: The bear had been wounded. Dawson's shot had hit home, but not in a fatal or even greatly damaging spot. It probably had served only to cause the bear to charge its tormentor. A stupid thing to do, he told himself, taking that shot at a target he couldn't even see.

Shortly the bear went over and began nosing around the deer carcass. It had been two hours and more now since the kill had been made. The bear's appetite had not been served. It began to feed, ripping and tearing at the flesh; but after a few minutes even this activity became halfhearted. Maybe the wound was bothering the animal, maybe it had not forgotten the man in the tree. It rose, then settled on all fours and shuffled back over to the tree, looking upward, then all around. Suddenly it came across something on the ground, nosed it cautiously for a few moments, then began to cuff at it. It had grown too dark for the man in the tree to see what the object was, but presently he heard the clatter of steel on rocks. *The rifle! The bear was cuffing the rifle off into the brush—just as if it knew what the thing was!*

Dawson Riddle tightened his grip on the tree trunk.

Finally the last faint glow of daylight faded; full darkness settled. There was no moon, not for another two hours at least, and then it would be well on the waning side of full. The bear became but a dark shape pacing round and round below, breathing hoarsely and on occasion issuing short, ill-tempered little grunts in an almost rhythmic fashion as it went. Or sometimes it would suddenly stop this and heave up on its hind legs, stretching high against the tree, ripping viciously at the bark with what was left of its front claws—ripping and tearing, growling and grunting. It would keep this up for several minutes, then once more drop to all fours.

"Go away, you old bastard," Dawson called down to it once. "Just go the hell away, for chrissake!"

At last the moon rose. The hillside brightened. The bear licked the wound on its haunch, returned to the deer carcass, and once again began to feed. Dawson heard a bone crunch and shivered, imagining it as one of his own. His legs and arms had long ago grown numb. His elbow, swollen now, ached terribly. A chill grew in the air. He tried for maybe the hundredth time to shift his position to one that was comfortable. There was no such position.

Midnight came and went. The bear had long since finished feeding. It came to scratch at the tree less and less frequently. It ceased pacing round and round the tree. It shuffled off a few yards, seeming to limp slightly now as its wound stiffened, and lay down. Night sounds came softly; the moon glowed; stars shone brightly.

Suddenly the bear got to its feet, shuffled back to the tree, looked up, its little eyes gleaming in the moonlight. For maybe a minute it stood there like that. Then it dropped its head and turned to what was left of the carcass, worked for a few moments to get a proper grip with its powerful jaws, and then began to drag its burden off across the clearing.

Dawson Riddle, who so far hadn't so much as thought of sleeping, watched in fascination as the huge animal made its way across the small clearing, going uphill. At the brush edge, it dropped the carcass and paused to look back at the tree, its body as if coated with shimmering frost there in the soft moonlight. For an instant it raised its nose to the air, sniffing. Then abruptly it turned, picked up the carcass once more, and left the clearing.

The man in the tree listened to the animal move through the brush until he could hear the sounds no more, then heaved a tremendous sigh of relief. The bear was gone. The question now was: Would it come back? Dawson did not have the answer, but one thing he did know was that he, Dawson Riddle, had no intention of taking any more chances than already had been taken. He

remained in the tree and did not come down until full daylight
had once again come upon the land.

3

June Greer stepped outside the cabin into a glaring early-after-
noon sun. Another hot, dry day seemed in store for them, just as
had been the case for most of the month so far. Still, she cast a
hopeful eye skyward. Scattered clouds were finally merging in the
east, which was at least promising of an afternoon shower someplace. She knew Gil would be glad for even such a tentative sign
as this that the normal summer rainy season was approaching.

Of course Gil wasn't at the ranch just then; he, Sir Robert, and
Sir Henry had only a few days before ridden out, the pretty white-
and-black setter trailing at their heels and another hunt on their
minds. Only the three of them had gone this time, Jessica having
lived up to her word to remain behind, and Anson Leggitt having
happily hastened to do the same. The hunters were not expected
back for several more days, and at present only the four women,
Leggitt, and Buck Blaine remained at the ranch.

The noon meal having been finished an hour ago, Buck had
gone up the hill to cut a few more poles for some finishing
touches on one of the corral gates, and surprisingly—perhaps out
of boredom, June thought—Anson Leggitt had offered to go along
and help. Shortly thereafter, Lady Greenstreet and Lady Gatlin,
followed by Jessica, had retired to their tents for an afternoon
nap, thus leaving June to herself for a while.

For a few moments the girl simply stood there, debating what
she might do with the time. She didn't really feel like lying down,
yet it was too hot to do a great deal else.

Thoughtfully she let her eyes roam out across the meadows.
Across the creek, half a dozen of Gil's cows lay, or stood lazily
swishing flies, beneath a lone pine tree at meadow's edge. Up a
winding sidecanyon beyond this, five or six others grazed along
the canyon's grassy bottom. At the head of the canyon, a high,
scrub oak-covered, conical-shaped hill Gil called Sugarloaf rose
haughtily and was particularly marked in appearance by its almost

complete lack of trees. Down by the barn, several horses stood side by side, each horse facing a direction opposite its partner's, tails swishing angrily at the deer and horse flies that plagued the animals constantly. And just past the barn, in a curve in the road, a lone horseman appeared abruptly, coming toward the house.

At first June had no idea who the rider could be and was even a little alarmed at his sudden appearance. Then, as he drew nearer, she recognized who he was. She waited as he rode up to the cabin and dismounted.

"Hello, Garst," she said as he tied his horse. "I didn't recognize you at first."

He tipped his hat and looked around. "Afternoon, June. Where is everybody?" Already his eyes had settled on the strange assemblage of tents nearby.

"The ladies are taking their afternoon naps," June told him a bit wryly. "Buck and Anson Leggitt are up the hill cutting corral poles, and Gil and the two Englishmen are off on another hunt for the bear."

The rancher wagged his head. "Those Englishmen don't give up, do they? They still think they can bring that old reprobate of a bear in, I suppose."

"I suppose."

Cunningham fidgeted a bit then. "Aren't you going to ask me in out of the sun?"

June looked back toward the cookshack hesitantly, then sighed. "Yes. Yes, of course. I didn't mean to be inhospitable. What brings you this time, Garst? Is there news from town? Have you seen my mother lately?"

"As a matter of fact, I have," he said as he followed her inside and took off his hat. She motioned toward a chair at the dinner table, which he took only after she had moved to take a seat across from him. "Just yesterday, I stopped by the cafe. Your mother asked me to come by if I got the chance and see how you were doing. I figure she's a bit worried about you. . . . You'd expect that, of course."

June acknowledged this with a nod. "Is she all right? Has she enough help at the cafe?"

"Oh, yeah, sure," he said. "Everything's fine on that score. But what I figure she's afraid of is that those Englishmen may not get the bear, that this thing'll drag on all summer and so will your stay here. Which is understandable, since she's probably right. I don't think there's a chance under the sun those crazy foreigners will get Old Tuffy, not one in a hundred."

June only shrugged. "They'll never know unless they try, will they?"

"No, I reckon not," he admitted grudgingly. "But I still think they're wasting their time. It'll take better than them to bring that old bear in, a lot better."

June bristled slightly at what she perceived was at least some reflection on Gil's ability to lead them. "How do you know that, Garst? Do you know anyone who's done any better so far? Anyone at all?"

Cunningham almost looked as if he had been waiting for this question. He said expansively, "Well, Dawson Riddle darned near landed the old devil here recently. He might be one who has. Or haven't you heard about that yet?"

"Heard about it?" June was completely puzzled. "No. I have no idea what you're talking about. Dawson Riddle almost got the bear? When?"

The rancher leaned back. "Oh, a week, ten days ago now, I guess. He was in town just a couple of days ago telling about it. He almost did it, June. Came within an eyelash of it, in fact."

June eyed him doubtfully. "Where? How?"

"Somewhere south of Squaretop, I reckon. According to him, he found the bear's tracks, then a kill it had made, and finally the bear itself. Trouble was, it was late in the day and he couldn't get a clean shot. He fired once, then lost his balance when the bear charged him and lost his rifle. He had to climb a tree to keep from getting mauled. But he hit it, June . . . would've brought it down if he hadn't had the bad luck of losing the rifle. He swears he would have."

June still looked skeptical. "But he didn't, did he? He didn't bring it down. And from the way it sounds, Dawson is probably lucky he survived. Isn't that right?"

"Yeah, yeah," the rancher admitted. "I suppose it is. But the point is, Dawson did locate the bear. He found its tracks and trailed it till he found it. Gil and those English dudes, now—have they even done that well? Have they, June?"

She shrugged. "I don't know. This is only their second time out. Who knows how things will go this time, or the next? If Dawson can get lucky, so can they. That's the way I see it."

"They'll have to," Cunningham concluded positively. "They'll have to be lucky to find the bear, and they'll have to be lucky not to get killed if they do find it. You can take my word for that."

June frowned. He had said this harshly, and she didn't like thinking about it that way, had worked very hard not to have to, in fact. Now Garst was forcing it on her in bold-faced terms figuratively ringing with irrefutability. She shook her head unhappily.

"Well, I shouldn't have said it that way, I guess," Cunningham said, divining her reaction. "It's not what I rode over here to talk to you about, really."

She eyed him cautiously. "Well, now, just what did you come to talk to me about? To check up on me for my mother, of course, but . . ."

He was looking down at his hands somewhat self-consciously now, hesitating, unsure. "Partly that, sure. But there's more. Your mother . . . well, your mother and I . . . we talked quite a lot yesterday. We, uh, think you should come back to town. We just sort of . . . I mean, I—"

June's eyes flashed irritably. "We? *We* think, Garst? You and my mother have made some sort of pact between you now, to look after my well-being or something? Is that it, Garst?"

"No . . . I mean, well, not exactly. It's just that I . . . Aw, hell, June. You know how I feel about you. It's not like I've got no right to be concerned—"

"You've got no right to interfere, Garst. With or without my mother's blessing, you've got no right to interfere with my life. What I'm doing here, what I'm doing anywhere, is my own business. I don't need you to be concerned about me, Garst. I can take care of myself."

He stared at her for a long moment, then straightened. "You don't *want* me to be concerned about you. That's what you really mean, isn't it? You don't want *me!*"

June sighed. Again he was forcing her to face something her instinct would have had her avoid. But she knew she couldn't do that, had long known that the time would one day come when she would have to say the inevitable to him.

She reached across and put a hand on one of his. "Garst, please understand. I do not dislike you; I value your friendship. You know I do, and I think you know too that I don't want to lose it. But that's all there is between us, Garst. It can't be anything more. Can't you see that?"

"It's Whitney, isn't it?" the man asked, unable to keep both frustration and anger from showing in his eyes and voice. "You're choosing Whitney over me. That's what you're saying."

"Perhaps I am, Garst. But nothing would change, with or without Gil. Please believe that. I just can't feel about you the way you want me to feel."

It was not an easy thing for him to accept. "You make a mistake, June," he insisted. "You pick the wrong man. You take hardscrabble, here, over success. Your ma sees that. You oughta."

"Gil won't always be hardscrabble, Garst. I know he won't."

"Oh, yeah? And just how do you know that?"

"Because all he needs is enough money ahead to buy a larger seed herd of better stock, enough to make it possible to turn these meadows into hayfields so he can winter his cattle properly. Money he'll have when he's finished guiding the Englishmen—especially if they get the bear. You know they've promised him all of the bounty money, don't you?"

Garst Cunningham rose from his chair, a look of disgust on his face. "A larger seed herd of better stock? Hay to feed them with? Good Lord, June, don't you know something's impractical when you hear it? Whitney's a dreamer, by damn—a dreamer and nothing more!"

June also rose. "You're wrong, Garst. Those are things you should be thinking about, too. I know enough about what's happened to the cattle industry in the past few years to see that. Surely you do, too."

He shook his head angrily. "Well, I can see I'm wasting my time here today. But I'm not giving up. Sooner or later you'll see I'm right. I'll be around still when that happens."

Silently she followed him out the door, watching as he untied and then mounted his horse in a single, swift movement.

"You mark my words, June," he told her. "Whitney'll starve out here, he'll starve out good. And if it's that bear bounty he's depending on to buy his seed herd and turn his meadows into hayfields . . . well, I can guarantee you he'll never see a dime of *that!*"

Without giving the startled girl a chance to respond, he reined his horse harshly around and spurred it into a trot, going back down the road the way he had come.

June watched until he had passed from view beyond the barn. Then, her brow set in a worried frown, she turned back to the cabin. Trying desperately to decide what he had meant by that parting remark, she just could not convince herself that what had sounded so very much like a threat was also an empty one.

4

She decided against worrying Gil about that last remark made by Cunningham when she told him of the other rancher's visit upon the hunting party's return to the ranch a few days later. They talked about it after supper that evening, and it was plain that Gil was deeply bothered at having once again failed not only to find the bear, but this time to locate even the faintest trace of it.

She mentioned what Garst Cunningham had said about Dawson Riddle encountering the grizzly only because she thought it would help if Gil knew approximately where that encounter had occurred.

" 'Somewhere south of Squaretop,' was the way Garst put it," she told him. "He said Dawson found tracks, then where a kill had been made, and then the bear. He apparently got off one shot and even wounded the animal before somehow losing both his balance and his rifle. He wound up climbing a tree to keep from getting mauled. But the thing is, he found the bear in the same general area where you thought Old Tuffy might be."

He nodded his head. " 'South of Squaretop' covers a lot of territory, June, all miles from here. That's the problem. We're having to hunt country too far from the ranch. It takes a full day just to get to some of it and get set up."

"Which means?"

"It's making it too hard. To do any good, we need to stay out longer."

She viewed this a bit unhappily. "You were out over a week this time!"

"I know. And we spent too much time traveling, too little hunting. And yet, Sir Robert and Sir Henry are both hesitant to leave the rest of their group here with nothing to do for much longer than that. They're worried that the women are going to grow bored with the whole thing and want to go home before the bear is found."

They had brought with them two chairs from the cabin and were sitting in front of the breezeway, facing the sunset. A soft footstep behind them might have gone unnoticed had it not been for the voice that accompanied it.

"And worried they should be!" Jessica St. John announced as she stepped around where they could see her. She had an apologetic look on her face. "I'm sorry. I couldn't help overhearing— but Gil, I am serious. It is a little much, just lying around here all day, every day, with you men gone and nothing to do. Wouldn't you agree, June?"

June shifted uneasily in her chair. "Well, yes, I suppose I do agree. But I'm surprised you would feel very strongly that way. After all, you have Anson. . . ."

Jessica smiled somewhat thinly. "I think you know that Anson is not always the comfort he cracks himself up to be." She laughed lightly, then looked around, ostensibly concerned that the remark might have been overheard. No one else was in sight, however, and probably already knowing that this would be the case, she turned back to Gil and June. "Anyway, I didn't mean just me. Elizabeth and Laura have both been a little edgy of late. June, you have too, I believe. And Anson has even been driven to do some work with Buck at times, he's so bored. Can you believe that?"

With a sigh, Gil rose and proffered his chair. "Well, I guess this is something we ought to talk about, all right. Sit down, Jessica. I'll go get another chair for me. Where did everyone else go?"

Jessica shrugged as she took the chair. "For a walk up the hill, I think. Everyone except Buck. I believe he's down at the barn. And Anson is doing something inside his tent—I have no idea what."

Gil went inside the cabin and presently returned with another chair. When seated again, he said, "Okay, girls. What about this getting bored business? Any ideas what to do about it?"

June, feeling a bit upstaged already by Jessica, only shrugged. The other girl hesitated over the cue only momentarily, then said, "It's simple, Gil—we need something to do. I realize that it may be—is!—asking more of you than what you bargained for, but isn't there some way we can all be a little closer to the action?"

Gil pondered this with no outward enthusiasm. "I thought we weren't going to have women going out on any more hunts. I thought we'd agreed on the reasons for that."

"We have," the girl admitted quickly. "And I don't mean to renege on a promise, either. But do you remember what *you* promised me? Do you remember what I asked of you after my one hunt?"

Gil frowned and so did June, who had no knowledge whatsoever that either a request or a promise had been made.

"I asked you to take me . . . us . . . all of us, if the others want to go, for a horseback ride or maybe even a short fishing trip. I thought maybe that would help break the monotony. We could go between hunts, of course. You said you would, and yet never did, remember?"

Slowly he nodded. "Yes. Yes, I remember. And I guess something like that would ease the problems here some. But it wouldn't solve my other problem—that of the bear. It doesn't give us any more time to hunt, and it might even cut in on what time we already have. And I owe it to Sir Robert and Sir Henry to make sure that doesn't happen. They're paying me to guide them to the bear, not to provide recreation for the hunting party!"

Jessica weighed this briefly. "Well, I know that, of course. And I perhaps shouldn't be speaking for anyone other than myself; naturally, the others should be consulted. But I do know that the problem here at the ranch exists." She paused. "June, don't you have any ideas?"

"Well," June started uncertainly, "I suppose there should be some way to tie the two things together. Like you say, Gil: The ranch just seems to be too far removed from where the hunt must take place. Some of the trips back and forth need to be eliminated. Maybe if the main camp were moved closer to the mountains. Maybe then you could get in the necessary time hunting the bear, while the rest of us would benefit from a change of scenery and maybe some time for fishing, and certainly we wouldn't be alone so much."

Gil felt initially a bit horrified as he looked over at the tents and thought about all of the supplies and equipment and accessories involved. "You mean pack this whole mess up and move it? Probably horseback over rough country—the women, too?"

June shrugged. "It's only a notion, Gil. Not a recommendation."

He looked at Jessica, who seemed suddenly quite excited. "Why, I think it's a wonderful proposal, Gil. We women wouldn't be directly involved in the hunt, but we wouldn't be so isolated from things as we are here, either. It would be adventure enough that we certainly would be well occupied, and you, meanwhile, would be free of all this riding back and forth. Think about it, Gil. Why wouldn't it work?"

Gil just stared from one to the other of them, shaking his head. Finally he said, "Have either of you any idea how much work such a thing might entail? Moving the camp fifteen miles or more over country where no wagon can go? Why, I doubt if we'd even be able to manage the big tents; you ladies would probably have to settle for the one-man type, bedrolls instead of cots, camp cooking instead of what you're getting at the cookshack now, a long horseback ride there and back—"

Jessica's smile was just short of a laugh. "Gil, I've been *through* all that already, remember? And I'm sure June would be up to it" —she shot June a somewhat challenging look—"wouldn't you, dear? As for Elizabeth and Laura, well, I think you know by now they are a spunky pair despite their titles. Come on, Gil—consider it, at least!"

"I don't know," he said hesitantly. "I just don't know. . . ."

"I'm sure we'll have to talk to the others first, Jessica," June interceded sympathetically. "Let Gil explain the problems, the inconveniences; let the others have a chance to decide."

"Of course. I agree. Wait here—I'll go find them and bring them here. You can make a list of all those problems and inconveniences while I'm gone, then we'll talk more about it. Okay, Gil?"

June watched the other girl go, then turned thoughtfully back to Gil. "I'm sorry, Gil. Maybe I shouldn't have said anything. But really—how can you be sure it's not a good idea? I think it might even be sort of fun. After all, even a bear hunt doesn't have to be all work and no play, does it?" She looked straight at him. "Well, *does it?*"

5

The two English ladies—inconvenience and hardship be hanged —loved the idea almost immediately. Sir Robert and Sir Henry considered it, asked a few questions, and decided jointly that perhaps the advantages would outweigh the disadvantages enough to make it worthwhile. Anson Leggitt predictably deplored it, but he argued little in the face of almost certainly being outvoted anyway. June agreed to go along with the majority's decision. Buck simply nodded his head and mumbled something to the effect that he didn't care what they did, so long as he was left to get some ranch work done while they were gone. Gil, eventually rendered bereft of an effective argument against the proposal, was left with nothing to do but agree that if most of them really wanted it to work out, then maybe it would.

"We'll have to do some work to get ready first, though," he warned them. "We'll even have to rebuild our stock of supplies some. My suggestion is that we wait until a day or so before the Fourth of July—less than a week away now, by my calendar—and maybe even spend a few days in town in the process. We can take a wagon and the two surreys, rest up a bit, and enjoy civilization for a few days, then come back here and get ready to go. You can see your mother, June, and maybe I can hire a chore boy to help out with the camp—assuming you still want to make the trip, that is."

"No way I'd miss it, Gil," the girl said, "it being my idea and all. No way."

"Not even if your mother says no?"

"My mother won't say no," she said confidently. "She may not like it, but she won't say no. Believe me."

They made the trip to town three days later; June drove one surrey, Buck the other. Gil handled one of the wagons, while the hunting party rode split up as passengers among the three vehicles. They stayed past the Fourth—on which it was traditionally supposed to rain, and did—went to a rodeo, bought supplies at Bud Sampson's store, hired a Mexican youth to do camp chores, stayed at the hotel (all except June, of course, who stayed with her mother), and ate at Mrs. Greer's cafe regularly. Both Garst Cunningham and Dawson Riddle were in town for the festivities, and Gil saw each at least twice but did not have occasion to talk to either of them. And as expected, June's mother made a concerted effort to talk June out of returning to the ranch, which—also as expected—failed. They loaded up and drove back to the ranch two days after the holiday, got rained on again, and spent the following day preparing for the trip into the mountains.

"We'll need a whole string of packhorses," Gil told them, "and we have a sidesaddle for each of you ladies who would prefer to ride one. Antonio"—the Mexican boy hired in town—"will be helping with the camp chores and the horses, while in camp, but everyone is going to have to help some. June, I'll help you and Jessica with the cooking whenever I'm around. Anson, you and Antonio will have to keep an eye out when Sir Robert, Sir Henry, and I are gone. Not a lot can happen to the women in camp, but some things can. Remember, we'll be up there to hunt grizzly, and the one we're after is not the only one around. There are grizzlies, lions, black bears—plenty of things to be cautious around. I am going to make sure someone is armed while we're gone—Antonio and June, at least, for they're both well acquainted with guns. The rest of you are not to get separated from at least one of those two. Most likely the worst you'll encounter are inconveniences, but likely that will include chiggers, ticks, mosquitoes, gnats, deer flies—all worse, if anything, than you've seen around the ranch here. There'll be skunks and porcupines, goose pimples at night and sunburns gained during the day, and undoubtedly we'll get rained on and soaked more than once. We'll have to wash our clothes in the river, and if you want to bathe, that'll have to be done in the river, too. Are you all sure you still want to go?"

"I never did want to go," Anson Leggitt spoke up, and was predictably ignored.

"It sounds like just what we came for, old chap," Sir Henry said, puffing happily on his pipe. "The more I think about it the more I think it'll be a bloody good show."

Buck, lounging nearby, looked skeptically past the Englishman. "How long you expect this 'bloody good show' to last, Gil? All summer?"

Gil smiled. "I doubt that. But if it's going to help the hunt any, it'll have to last however long that takes." He glanced over at a thoughtful Sir Robert. "Otherwise, I guess it will simply depend on the group and how much they can stand. Do you agree, Sir Robert?"

"We'll stand it, Whitney," the Englishman assured. "You can count on it."

Gil looked around the group. "Anybody else?"

Anson Leggitt looked up, almost spoke, then apparently decided to keep it to himself.

Lady Gatlin said, "Please don't worry so about our ability to take the hardships, Mr. Whitney. Once all that horseback riding is over, why, I'm sure we'll do just fine. Really we will."

"She's right," Lady Greenstreet put in. "Even the horseback ride shouldn't be all that difficult. I mean, fifteen miles or whatever it is shouldn't be so bad, should it?"

"In mountain country," Gil said, "it can be like fifty, anywhere else. So, I wouldn't take the ride lightly, ladies. You'll regret it if you do, believe me."

"You listen to what the man says, girls," Sir Robert told them. "Riding in that country is no picnic, I can attest to that!"

"But the point is, we *can* handle it," Jessica St. John interposed confidently. "I know we can."

"That's quite it, all right," Lady Gatlin added. *"Of course* we can!"

Gil wasn't fully reassured, however; and so the next day he readied them for the trip with every intention of maintaining a fully unhurried pace all the way to their high-country campsite. He had in mind a point along the Blanco River almost due south of Squaretop Mountain. They would reach the site via a route he considered somewhat roundabout but that was also as easy as any they might use to get there. Certainly the trail would not be as the crow flies, and with the women along it might take more than one day to traverse. But that was okay: He was prepared to be patient.

Drawn on a map, their itinerary might look something like the trail of a drunken snake. From the house they would first head east, past the upper meadows and the cottonwood grove, slanting only slightly southward as they made their way to the Little Blanco River. At the Little Blanco they would then turn almost due south, following the river all the way to its confluence with Sheep Cabin Creek. Crossing Sheep Cabin, they would once again go in an easterly direction, passing in the shadow of Bear Mountain as they worked their way over a low divide into the watershed of the "Big" Blanco. Upon their arrival at the Blanco, they would then travel upstream in the direction of the beautiful fir- and spruce-timbered basin, through which the early flowings of the river passed. There, along the Blanco, probably somewhere just past its confluence with Leche Creek, they would establish the main camp.

The location Gil was thinking of was quiet and secluded, very pretty, and would be as good a place to fish or hike or simply to relax as any they could choose. The spot would also be ideal as a headquarters for the bear hunters, for it was as perfectly centered within the big grizzly's range as anyplace known.

Still, it was an endeavor the likes of which Gil had never before undertaken. Nine people were involved, four of whom were women. Almost as many packhorses as saddle horses were required. Gil's main helpers, those with any real experience at all in such circumstances, were the Mexican boy, Antonio, and June. Sir Robert and Sir Henry had already proven that they were at least willing to carry their own weight, but they remained inexperienced in most facets of camping and hunting in the West. Jessica knew just enough to be of limited help. Anson Leggitt was little more than deadweight. The two English ladies had their spunk going for them, but were an unknown quantity otherwise. All would be basically dependent on Gil throughout, the dog, Fleck, being perhaps the only other member of the party that could operate self-sufficiently if it came down to that.

As they prepared to ride out from the ranch, Gil told Buck, "Look for us back when you see us coming, I guess."

"And if I don't see you," the older man asked with a keen look, "how long do I wait to go looking for you?"

"Well," Gil said after a moment's deliberation, "the only thing I can think of is . . . if Dawson Riddle comes in with the bear while we're still out there . . . then for sure, you come and get us!"

It was perhaps prophetic that Gil thought of Dawson Riddle just then. As the hunting party rode out, Riddle and Garst Cunningham sat undetected on a section of the north ridge, watching intently. They had left the Cunningham ranch shortly after sunup and had been on the ridge ever since the hunting party had begun saddling up. They had with them two packhorses of their own.

"D'you ever see anything like that before?" Dawson Riddle said as he watched.

Cunningham's jaw was as tight as stretched hemp. "Nine riders and eight packhorses. All four women, two of them riding astride —that'll be June and probably the St. John woman. . . . No, Dawson, I've never seen that many fools in one bunch before. Never."

"Where d'you reckon they'll go?"

Cunningham shrugged. "All I know is, Mrs. Greer told me they were planning to set up camp along the Blanco, somewhere south of Squaretop."

"Are we still gonna follow 'em?"

"Yes."

Riddle cocked his head. "How come? is what I don't figure. What difference does it make to us where they go?"

"We're going after the bear, just like they are. We'll probably find ourselves hunting in the same general vicinity, and I just figure we ought to know where they are, is all."

Dawson Riddle shook his head. He knew there was more to it than that, but he could see that Cunningham was determined to be noncommittal about it. Not that Dawson was really all that fooled by the situation. He knew it had something to do with that Greer girl—good old Garst had a passion for that one, he did. Maybe even more so than what he had for bringing in the bear. But that was all right as far as Dawson was concerned. They were still going after the bear. It was the bear that counted, after all.

The hunting party finally passed from view beyond the cottonwood grove, leaving only one person behind at the ranch. "Buck didn't go," Cunningham commented with a satisfied look. "That's one good thing."

"Why d'you say that?" Dawson asked.

Cunningham didn't even look at him. "Because the less real help Whitney has, the harder it's going to be for him to put those Englishmen onto the bear, that's why."

Dawson frowned. "Well, that's all right with me, but what difference does it make to you? I thought you said you didn't care who got the bear, so long as somebody did."

"Things change," Cunningham said tautly. "I care now. I want us to get him, no one else." He gave Dawson a look this time. "Do you understand that?"

"Yeah, sure. I guess so." Dawson shrugged. What the hell.

Presently they started down from the ridge, angling toward a point upcanyon from the cottonwood grove, avoiding the house. They were in no hurry and were if anything more concerned with not being seen than they were with falling too far behind. They would have no trouble picking up the trail of nine riders and eight packhorses, they knew.

6

*There seemed no end to the things people had tried on the
bear. One of the most effective methods of putting an end to trou-
blesome grizzlies was also one of the simplest—and most dis-
tasteful. Many times, it was resorted to only after all else had
failed. A homesteader named Cutler, who five years back had located himself down by the Little Navajo River well to the south
of the basin, had come to the end of his rope with the bear early
on in the game.*

*Over a summer's time he had lost—or at least perceived to have
lost—two colts, his best work mule, and no fewer than half a
dozen calves to the big grizzly. He had tried hunting the beast—
tracking, stalking, still hunting near caches, berry patches, deer
runs, and regularly used bear trails—and had failed at every turn.
Primarily a farmer, he didn't have enough stock to absorb these
kinds of losses and still survive as a homesteader, and by late summer was feeling truly desperate.*

*One pleasant September day he rode the twenty or so miles it
took him to get to town, and returned the following day with a
few supplies he had been needing plus a liberal supply of strychnine. This he carried with him everywhere he rode for the better
part of the next month. And he rode a lot—all over, from Navajo
Peak to the east of his place to Squaretop, well to the north. He
rode and he rode, looking endlessly for sign of the big grizzly.*

*Finally he found what he was looking for: A fresh kill, a year-
ling elk downed near the Big Branch tributary to the Blanco, with
the familiar tracks of a huge bear everywhere around it. The carcass had been partially eaten, then half covered over with leaves
and twigs and dirt. The intent of the bear to return for a second
meal seemed clear. Careful not to disturb anything, Cutler approached the carcass and proceeded to apply what he considered a
more than adequate dose of the bitter strychnine to it. Then he
returned to his horse and rode away.*

*It was late in the day and he did not go far; he made camp less
than a mile away. Convinced that the bear would most likely*

*revisit its kill during the night, he wanted to return to the site
early the next day to inspect what had happened. He considered
the poison approach almost foolproof under such circumstances
and was so keyed up over the prospect of having put an end to the
bear he almost couldn't sleep that night.*

*He was up at the first pale light of dawn, but he did not hasten
straightaway to the site of the poisoned cache. He let the sun rise
well into the sky, afraid to risk even the slightest chance of disturbing the bear during an early-morning feeding. But after a
while he could wait no longer; he saddled his horse, cleaned up his
camp, and rode out at a leisurely pace, calculating his arrival at
the cache at about ten o'clock. On his way there, he came upon a
fresh paw print entering the trail, one he was sure had been made
since Cutler himself had passed the same way going toward his
night camp yesterday. A quick inspection proved him right, and if
this wasn't source enough for excitement, the fact that the bear
was headed in the direction of the cache surely was.*

*Almost breathlessly Cutler proceeded on up the trail, and when
he came within sight of the small mound that was the remains of
the carcass, he pulled up nervously. For a full minute he surveyed
the area. He did not see the bear, but its tracks were still there in
front of him, headed straight for the carcass. Finally Cutler eased
his horse forward.*

*As he drew up to the cache, he realized with some disap-
pointment that the carcass appeared undisturbed. It seemed to lie
exactly as he had left it, leaves and dirt partially covering it just as
before. But how could that be? The bear's paw prints were all
over the place, many of which had plainly been made since
Cutler's visit to the carcass yesterday. Could the animal have returned only to pass up the very feast it had come back to enjoy?*

*Cutler dismounted and started to study the tracks. The big griz-
zly had circled the carcass widely several times, as if inspecting it.
But clearly it had not fed. Had it detected something wrong?
Surely not the poison . . . the man at the store in town had assured him the bear would not know until too late that the strychnine had been applied. Could it have been Cutler's own scent?
Plainly the animal hadn't been afraid to approach just because of
that . . . so, why would it not eat? Cutler shook his head. No bear*

was smart enough to be so leery when it meant passing up a well-earned meal. No bear. . . .

And then he saw something he should have seen before, and he knew that this bear, at least, had figured something out. Perhaps it had even determined what was wrong with the carcass! As unlikely as this seemed, homesteader Cutler could only shake his head at what he saw.

Half-concealed there in the leaves and dirt, located squarely atop the carcass and laced with undigested berry seeds, lay a large pile of excrement. Whether or not the act had been the bear's way of saying what it thought of someone messing around with its kill was a matter of pure conjecture. But to Cutler, at least, it hardly seemed an accident that the pile had been deposited exactly where it lay!

Later that fall, before the first big snow could catch him, he packed up his belongings and moved his homestead out of the mountains, all the way to Colorado's eastern plains—which he had now decided were a good deal more hospitable toward farmers than the Little Navajo country, anyway.

CHAPTER 4

THE BASIN

1

Among them, only Gil had ever before witnessed such pristinely beautiful surroundings. Even Sir Robert's many excursions had not taken him to another spot so pleasantly secluded. The basin simply had not been settled yet, and the river that tumbled and gurgled down its center yielded water as pure as any stream ever could. It was every bit the wild, raw environment it had been made out to be.

Camp had been made three days earlier among towering spruce and fir, within fifty yards of the river's bank, and it had rained each day since. Not all day, not even particularly hard, just steady mountain showers mostly, coming each afternoon along about two or three o'clock and lasting anywhere from half an hour to two hours. But following each rain lingered the cleanest, clearest air known to man, and the land was refreshed. The smell of live and growing vegetation was strongly pleasant everywhere; grasses greened noticeably and flowers—blue-, white-, and scarlet-petaled —abounded and became more beautiful with each passing day; small animals and birds scurried and flitted about, invigorated; elk and deer grazed within fifty yards of camp each morning and evening, mingling at times with the horse herd; small, dark-bodied trout darted and flashed in the river's pools, and submitted to an angler's hook only after the most desperate of battles had been fought to remain free. It was a world in which there seemed little likelihood of anything ever going wrong.

They were about three miles south and slightly east of Square-top Mountain. The camp faced generally south, toward the river, and consisted of a tent for each of the women and tarp-covered bedrolls for the men. It was just after sundown that third day, supper having been finished only minutes earlier. Gil sat by the fire, built of half-dry wood found earlier in the day and protected beneath a tarp-covered lean-to from the afternoon's showers. The horses, hobbled, grazed nearby under the watchful eye of the Mexican boy, Antonio. June and Jessica were down at the river washing supper dishes and utensils. Anson Leggitt and the two English ladies had gone for a walk, while Sir Robert and Sir Henry sat across from Gil, sipping gingerly from cups of hot tea.

"Well, what say, Whitney?" Sir Robert asked presently. "Is the camp settled enough now that we can make a bit of a hunt to-morrow?"

Gil nodded. "I think so. At least I figure we can get in a good day and still be back by supper. Things ought to be all right here for that length of time."

"I believe so, too," Sir Henry said, methodically filling his pipe bowl with tobacco. "Which way will we go?"

Gil leaned back as Fleck came from somewhere behind one of the tents and lay down at his side. He looked toward the mountains beyond the river. "I'm thinking to cross the river here, swing northeastward toward what's called Fish Creek, then come back along the footslopes of Flattop Mountain. It's anybody's guess where the bear might be at this time of year, but that's as good a place as any to start."

"What if we don't find anything thereabouts? What then?"

Gil shrugged. "Well, we might work south toward the Little Navajo. The bear's been known to favor that area as summer wears on—at least so say a couple of ranchers down that way."

"Can we go that far and still make it back here in one day?" Sir Robert asked.

"To the Little Navajo? Probably not. But we won't need to worry about that for a while. I want to concentrate on the area around here until we're reasonably sure there's nothing to be found closer in. Who knows, if Dawson Riddle's account of how he located the bear this side of Squaretop is true, maybe we've as good a chance as any right here in the basin."

"But if we have to expand the search, we go south . . . is that it?"

"That's my opinion, yes."

"You don't think your Riddle chap might have frightened the bear out of this area? Wasn't the story that he actually wounded it or something?"

"That's what Garst Cunningham told June," Gil admitted. "But apparently the bear wasn't bad hurt by it, and if anyone got really scared, I think it was Dawson." He smiled, then went on. "Of course that doesn't mean the bear might not move on. It probably did. But in country like this, a few miles away can be a whole new territory. I don't look for the animal to abandon the area it knows best just because of Dawson Riddle."

The two Englishmen exchanged looks. Sir Robert nodded and said, "You're the guide, Whitney, and I'm with you. What time tomorrow do we start?"

2

They left shortly after breakfast, but only after Gil had provided detailed instructions to those staying behind as to who should be responsible for what.

"Don't worry about us, Gil," June told him. "Antonio and I will keep both an eye on the others and our rifles handy. Maybe we'll even catch a few fish before you get back. How would a mess of pan-fried cutthroats sound to you for supper? Pretty good, huh?"

He smiled. June was a natural at fly fishing, and she had been like a kid with new toys the moment she had seen—and then been told she could use—a sample of the fancy fishing gear Sir Robert had brought along.

"It'd sound great," he said. "But if you want to catch any, you had better get a move on. You'll likely do no good in the heat of the day."

They crossed the river a short distance upstream from camp,

their horses' ironshod hoofs clattering in the cobbles as they went. Then they struck a trail that Gil knew would take them all the way to the tributary he called Fish Creek.

Climbing steadily, they soon left the river and the camp beyond view and made their way among dense stands of aspen, oak, and occasionally pine. Spruce and fir occurred here and there and would become even more prevalent higher up. Because both the ground and the vegetation were wet from yesterday's rain and this day's morning dew, only the most freshly made tracks would likely be seen on any trail.

Sir Robert evidenced some concern about this as they rode. "Will it hamper us or not, Whitney? I mean, all this mud?"

"In some ways, it might. We certainly won't be able to identify regularly used bear trails because of it. But on the other hand, there'll be no doubt how fresh a track is when we do find one. That part will be a plus. And don't worry. Things will dry out soon enough, as long as it doesn't rain again and the sun stays out. The main thing is finding a track—one we can follow that we know was made by our bear."

"What're the odds on that happening?" Sir Henry asked from behind Sir Robert. "Good or bad?"

"No way of knowing. We'll just have to ride and look and see what happens. Maybe we'll have some luck. Who knows?"

"Maybe we should have brought that setter of yours along," Sir Robert suggested. "Maybe he could put us onto a trail."

Gil shrugged. Although certainly not a trained bear dog, and prone at times to chase almost anything that would run, Fleck remained basically a well-mannered dog who was easily controlled by Gil. He had never been a liability on previous hunts and might even be of some help if they ever did get onto a hot trail. But Gil had left him behind this time, mostly for use as a warning device for June and the others in case anything at all untoward approached the camp while the hunters were gone. He still considered that the more worthwhile use of the dog.

"Not much even a trained bear dog can do, much less Fleck, unless we locate a fresh trail first," he told Sir Robert. "That's the first thing we've got to do—locate fresh sign."

They rode on, still climbing but more gradually now. It was a country of many small parks and meadows, of tiny creeks sometimes swelled into ponds by industriously constructed beaver dams, of tall, beautiful aspen and associated deadfalls, of variety upon variety of many-colored flowers and green grass, of stately conifers, of animals and birds both large and small, fearsome and fearful, noisy and quiet. They saw deer and elk slipping through the trees and brush; squirrels, chipmunks, rabbits, jays, magpies were everywhere; they heard a marmot whistling, woodpeckers tapping resoundingly, high up in this or that tall tree. They found tracks of all kinds, mostly deer and elk, but even those, once, of what Gil was certain was a mountain lion. They came across a chokecherry patch and found bear tracks and fresh scat, but the tracks were small and claw marks did not show in the front toe prints.

"Black bear," Sir Henry announced the second this was pointed out to him. "Yes, well, I do know something about that, all right. Just last night I was reading some notes old Gatlin here took one time from your Lewis and Clark Journals and some other references describing the grizzly bear." He paused, eyes bright with a knowledge he was obviously dying to impart. He repeated almost as if straight from the texts, although obviously paraphrasing: "Yes sir, legs longer than the black bear, talons and tusks much larger and longer, testicles placed farther forward . . . suspended in separate pouches from two to four inches asunder, while those of the black bear hang between the legs like those of a dog. Most common characteristics are small eyes and ears, dished-face, high shoulders, and those long, curved claws of the front feet *that ought to show in the tracks.* Yes sir. We are looking at black bear footprints, my friends. Henry Greenstreet knows *that* much!"

Gil and Sir Robert both laughed, and Gil said, "I think you're right, Sir Henry. Most likely a medium-sized black bear at best, and certainly not Old Tuffy."

"But at least it's a bear," the jaunty little Englishman said. "By Jove, that's some progress, isn't it?"

"Yes . . . some," Gil said, then added only to himself, *but not much. Not very much at all.* Finding a chokecherry patch with black bear tracks in it was nothing uncommon; finding those of a certain very special grizzly was something else entirely.

They came to the upper reaches of Fish Creek along about noon, lunched, and then began following a trail upstream that would lead eventually to the backside of Flattop Mountain. Gil hesitated to pursue this route too far, for fear they might not be able to make it back to camp by dark. He much preferred a rather rugged but shorter branch in the trail that would curl sharply across the mountain's footslopes on its north side (the side they were now on), and from there take them back in the direction of the Blanco, whence they had come. Getting back by dark would not be easy, even then, but since they were unencumbered by packhorses and had a downhill go most of the way, he figured it would work out about right. And they would have been covering good bear country from beginning to end. It was as good a way to go as any, he knew—if they could just find some sign of the bear. Some sign, any sign at all. . . .

But they did not. They looked long and hard, observed every other kind of sign imaginable, and discovered nothing of the Great Silver Bear. What they did find of note, however, gave them— Gil, at least—reason for a good deal of pause.

They were almost back in camp when, on a long, sweeping slope leading toward the river, they came upon four distinct sets of horse tracks, all shod, and two sets of boot prints. There was no possible way the tracks could be any of their own, and when they got to camp but a quick few questions were necessary to ascertain that none of the group left behind had gone out during the day.

"What do you think, Whitney? Does it mean something?" Sir Robert asked, wondering mostly, it seemed, at Gil's own concerned expression.

"I don't know." Gil's eyes were fixed narrowly back on the slope where they had found the tracks. "Except those tracks were made either late yesterday after the rain or early this morning before the ground started to dry. And whoever it was stayed on that hill for some while before moving on. There were at least two riders, they were there long enough to dismount and tie their horses, and they had one helluva good view of this camp."

"You think they were watching us?" The Englishman was a bit wide-eyed now.

"Probably, yes."

"But why?"

"I have no idea."

"Maybe they were just passersby," June suggested. "Maybe they saw our camp and were curious. Maybe they watched awhile, then continued on their way."

Gil looked at her. "But why didn't they come on down and say hello? That would've been the customary thing to do."

"I don't know, Gil." The girl shrugged. "Maybe they just didn't want to come so far out of their way."

He thought about it as his eyes swerved back to the slope. "Maybe so," he said after a moment. But the more he thought about it later, the more he doubted that this could be the case. Folks just didn't do that in this part of the country. He was convinced that if their business up on that hillside had been innocent, they would have come on down to say hello.

3

The dog woke the camp sometime past midnight two days later. Gil and the two Englishmen had come in after dark, excited at having made two separate sightings of grizzlies during the day—one of which had been seen at some distance just before dark and had definitely looked large enough to be Old Tuffy. The animal had been too far away and full dark too near to investigate further at the time, but the hunters had stayed up late discussing their plans for doing so early the next day.

Gil had been asleep little more than two or three hours when he came awake suddenly to the dog's barking. Sleepily, he scrambled from his bedroll and pulled on his boots. By the time he got to his feet, rifle in hand, both Sir Robert and Antonio were already at his side.

"What is it?" the Englishman asked as Sir Henry stirred in his bedroll and someone else showed a sleepy face between a pair of tent flaps. "What's the matter with your bloody dog, Whitney?"

Gil stared hard into the night. A growing half-moon had already disappeared over the western horizon and no longer yielded any light. He could make out nothing. "Something's out there," he said nevertheless. "Around the horses, I think. Antonio, do you see anything?"

The boy shook his head. Dim forms took shape, moving in the foreground toward the river; horses snorted; hoofs stamped. From somewhere among the horses, the dog barked even more wildly than before. Sir Henry came to stand beside the others, and Anson Leggitt moaned from his bedroll. "Get some light," Gil called to Antonio, who had moved a few feet ahead now. "There's a bull's-eye lantern over by the fire pit."

The boy hustled to do as he was told. But even before he could locate a match with which to light the lantern, the sound of hoofs clattering on rocks and splashing in the river came to them.

"Jesus," Gil muttered. "The horses are loose. Come on, Sir Robert—bring your rifle! Sir Henry, grab a couple of lariat ropes!"

He started running, saw some of the horses now and finally something white darting back and forth that he knew was Fleck, still barking. A horse charged past him, swerved toward the river, splashed across it. It ran unfettered. . . .

Gil thought he heard voices somewhere out there, and he knew they could not belong to any of the hunting party. Another horse lurched off to the right, this one still hobbled and unable to run. Steel-shod hoofs rang on rocks across the river now; a horse whinnied.

Footsteps sounded behind him; a bright beam of lantern light settled on the horse off to the right. The animal stood trembling and was indeed still hobbled. Sir Henry came running up with a pair of lariats, amazingly tangled. He proffered them to Gil. Separating the two ropes as quickly as he could, Gil handed his rifle to Sir Henry and one of the ropes to Antonio.

"Sir Robert, take the lantern! Antonio, catch that horse! I think I see another one still hobbled over there. . . ."

Fifteen minutes later they had captured two horses and had led them back to camp. The dog, soaking wet, had returned to camp now, still excited but no longer barking. As best they could tell, all of the other horses were gone into the night.

"How did it happen?" Sir Robert asked in consternation. "*What* happened? Was it the bear or something?"

Everyone stood around a rekindled campfire, the women either hurriedly dressed or having wrapped themselves in blankets, the men with pants and boots on but shirtless or with long underwear alone covering their upper torsos. Even Anson Leggitt stood wonderingly among them, also half-dressed.

Gil held a knife-cut piece of rope in one hand. "It wasn't a bear, Sir Robert. Those horses had their hobbles cut and were run off by someone who just didn't get to the two we caught. It was some*body* that did that. I'm sure I heard voices out there while the horses were still crossing the river."

"Good heavens!" The Englishman looked shocked, as did everyone else except Gil. "Who would *do* such a thing?"

"I have no idea," Gil said, "unless . . . unless maybe it was those two characters who watched the camp two days ago from across the river. . . . The tracks we saw—remember?"

The others exchanged looks. "Horsethieves, Gil?" June asked, eyes wide. "You think they were common horsethieves?"

"It's possible."

"But why did they wait two whole days, Gil?" the girl continued to wonder. "If it was those men who watched our camp, why now?"

"I don't know. Could be they were playing it cautious; could be it took two days for them to get their nerve up. I just don't know."

June looked thoughtful, troubled somehow. She seemed to have remembered something. "Gil . . . you don't suppose it could possibly have been . . ." She stopped, then shook her head vigorously. "No . . . no, surely not. It couldn't be."

"What, June?" Gil's eyes narrowed. "What are you suggesting?"

"Nothing . . . nothing at all." Again she shook her head. "I'm wrong, I must be wrong. Forget I said anything—please."

Gil studied her for a moment, then shrugged. "Well, anyway, we're lucky the dog woke us before whoever it was cut the hobbles on those last two horses. We'd really have been in a pickle without them!"

"But what will we do with only two?" Sir Henry asked. "Two blooming horses can't carry all of us!"

"No. Of course not. But they will make it possible for someone to go and look for the others."

Sir Robert eyed Gil skeptically. "You think we can find any of them, Whitney? You think we can actually get them back from those bloody horsethieves?"

Gil looked into the darkness, in the direction of the river. "I don't know, Sir Robert. But I do know this: Come morning, I am personally going to give it one helluva try. You can count on that!"

They staked out the two remaining horses within fifteen yards of the bedrolls and went back to bed. At the first gray light of day, Gil was up and starting breakfast; an hour later he had looked the two horses over and had selected the one he would ride. As luck would have it, the horse was the one assigned to June, a sturdy bay gelding that came from Gil's own horse herd at the ranch, one he himself had ridden many times and knew to be trustworthy. The other was one of the packhorses they had purchased in town, and Gil wasn't even sure it had been broken to ride.

"You're certain you won't let someone go with you?" Sir Robert asked as Gil saddled the bay. "You don't think you might need some help out there?"

"No. I'll take the dog with me and will otherwise probably do just as well alone. There is something else I could use some help with, though—if you think the group here might be willing."

"Oh? What's that?"

"You see that rock bluff over there?" Gil pointed to a spot about fifty yards away, where a massive vertical outcropping rose to thirty feet in height and extended at least a hundred feet across its face. "I'm thinking we could build a pole corral in front of that rock, using the bluff itself for the backside of the corral. We've plenty of axes and shovels, and there's a stand of aspen just beyond that will do for posts and poles. A few posts, thirty or forty good poles, and I think we could put together an adequate corral to hold our horse herd. Antonio will know how to go about it if some of you want to get started. I'll be back as soon as possible, hopefully with some of the horses, and then I can help finish it. If I can get some of them back, it'd give us a safe place to hold them from here on in, and maybe keep something like this from happening again. Do you think the group can handle it?"

Sir Robert never hesitated. "Handle it? Why, we'll more than handle it, old chap. Won't we, Henry? Anson? Of course we will. You just bring back those bloody horses, Whitney; we'll get to work on the corral."

June, then the other women, chimed in that they would help, and Antonio nodded confidently that he could show them what to do. "We'll use this packhorse to drag the poles, Mister Gil," the boy said. "And we'll do it pretty *pronto*, you'll see!"

Gil smiled and mounted the bay. "Keep an eye peeled and a rifle or two handy," he warned. "I don't think those jaspers from last night will come back, but let's don't take chances—okay?"

"Don't worry about that, Whitney," Sir Henry assured, hefting his firearm affectionately. "Just let those rotten blokes show their faces around here again. They'll bloody well wish they hadn't, I'll tell you!"

Gil left them there and crossed the river going in the direction he'd last seen or heard horses running last night, and quickly found plenty of tracks on the other side. At first the nature of the tracks seemed to reflect little more than mass confusion. But after a few minutes he was able to determine that most, if not all, of the animals had headed on downriver, and that they had gone apparently in a bunch, as if being driven. Since this did not surprise him, he moved out steadily to follow the tracks, the dog Fleck trotting along dutifully at his horse's heels.

The river serpentined along the base of its canyon in such a manner that in order to follow its course one was forced frequently to cross it. The horse tracks reflected this, and Gil could do no less than follow suit. There were too many tracks for him to attempt seriously to number their makers, but he knew he was looking for up to fifteen loose horses, and possibly two others with riders. Because of the latter possibility, he carried his rifle across his lap and kept his eyes peeled.

About a mile downstream, he began to wonder what manner of horsethieves these were when he came upon three of the camp's horses, grazing peacefully along the riverbank. They did not act wild and one even raised its head and nickered a friendly greeting to Gil's horse as it approached. Gil had carried with him two extra lariats and half a dozen bridles for just such an eventuality, and after working his way carefully up to the three he easily slipped a loop, then a bridle headstall, over the first horse's head. He dismounted, tied this horse to a nearby bush, and started after the other two. It took a bit more doing, but presently he had all three tied to bushes next to each other and was again on his way. With luck he would find more horses farther downriver and could pick these three up on the way back.

Of course it might not be so easy to find any others. If those men last night had indeed been horsethieves, they clearly would have been intent on driving the horses on off. That three had got by them in the night could hardly be classed as surprising. That many more might do so, however, would be.

Nevertheless, after another half a mile Gil came across five more horses, again grazing peacefully. Now Gil was truly wondering about the horsethieves. They had gone to an awful lot of trouble and some risk to drive the horses off, but they had allowed over half of them to get away from them already. *That* didn't make any sense at all.

Or did it? Gil surveyed the scene ahead very carefully. Could someone be waiting in ambush up there? Someone having set a careful trap, who was now waiting for him to come looking for his horses? Well, not likely, he decided. If they *were* just horsethieves, they would undoubtedly take their booty and run. They would avoid, not look for, a confrontation with their victims. *If* they really were only horsethieves. . . .

After several minutes he decided it was a safe gamble to go ahead. Only this time he did not try to catch any of the horses. A couple of them looked a little skittish as he approached, and he did not want them to take off on him. Ordering Fleck to stay close at his heels, he very carefully swung wide of them, intent on getting below them to a point at which he could then start them back in the direction of camp. Once started in the right direction, they should continue gradually on upriver, where he could always pick them up again later.

He got the five moving, then stopped to watch until he was satisfied with the way they were going. When indeed he was satisfied, he then reined his horse back around in the direction taken by the tracks of the remaining half a dozen or so animals. All were shod horses, still moving downriver, and Gil remained acutely aware that a couple of them might have been ridden by the horsethieves.

Just around the next bend in the river he came upon two more horses, once again grazing in an undisturbed manner. One of these was his own favorite saddle horse, a long-legged sorrel with blaze face and stockinged feet. The other was the roan gelding that was Sir Henry's. These, too, he got below and then drove for a ways back upriver. Again he stopped and watched them go. All told, this made ten of the missing fifteen horses accounted for. Ten of fifteen. He wondered anew at the horsethieves. Had they even got off with the remaining five? If so, it certainly hadn't been much of a haul. Some horsethieves!

Somehow there no longer remained five sets of tracks to follow, however. Without Gil noticing, one or more river crossings must have resulted in at least a couple of the horses having separated from the others and perhaps having left the river canyon altogether. In any case, at his feet now were only three sets of tracks, and nothing short of backtracking would discover where the others had gone. After some consideration of this fact, he decided to continue on after the three that remained.

A mile farther and he came upon one more horse—a pretty little sorrel one of the English ladies had ridden—that was so happy to see Gil's horse it came nickering at a gallop up to meet them the minute Gil came into sight. Gil didn't figure there was much use trying to drive a single horse anywhere, for it would probably turn around and follow him anywhere he went anyway. Thus he slipped a bridle over its head and decided to lead it along with him as he followed the remaining two sets of tracks downriver.

He did not think it odd that the horse was as excited as it was at seeing another horse; he knew that horses were often like that when separated from their companions.

Unfortunately this apparently was not all there was to the horse's nervousness. About a mile downstream he found what was for all practical purposes the end of the trail. He also found one of the horses that had made the tracks. Only this horse was not grazing peacefully along the riverbank, and it did not come galloping up to meet them. It was Fleck that raced forward and found it— lying on its side, dead for perhaps several hours. It lay covered with twigs and leaves and dirt, and but for the tracks and the dog, would not have been easy to find. The tracks of the second horse evidenced an animal taking off at a dead run toward the trees along the canyon's edge. They disappeared going west and gave no indication that the animal had soon slowed down.

Dismounting slowly at the carcass of the dead horse, Gil surveyed the scene all around it. A tremendous struggle was evidenced by the disturbance of the ground, a large pool of blood, and deep claw and tooth marks on the horse's back and neck, either of which or both could have been broken.

There was little doubt what had happened. Jagged chunks had been ripped from both haunches and the left flank; something very large had fed on its kill here and then had partially covered what was left. It had taken something large to kill a full-sized horse like this. Gil's heart raced as he guessed at what must have been the villain, even before he paused to study the telltale tracks.

They were clearly bear tracks, and they were enormous. Even before he looked to make sure, he suspected that certain toes would be missing on both front feet. He was not disappointed in this.

Two hours later he returned to camp driving eleven horses before him, a tremendous degree of excitement raging within him, and an almost complete loss of interest having been suffered in whoever had run the horses off the night before.

4

The corral was half finished by the end of the day. Gil wanted desperately to return to the site of the bear's most recent kill that night, but as reason returned he realized that the horses must first be protected from another such event as the previous night had produced. Each animal was to be staked and hobbled close by, and the men of the hunting party would divide up to provide a guard throughout the night. Tomorrow the corral would be finished and the horses could be more safely kept.

"You really believe someone ran those horses off for some reason other than to steal them?" Sir Robert asked Gil over supper. "They weren't just horsethieves?"

"If they were," Gil said soberly, "they were the most stupid horsethieves who ever lived. At most, they got away with three horses. Three out of seventeen. Now, what kind of horsethieves are those?"

"It was dark, Gil," June said then. "Maybe they could only manage three; maybe they never wanted more than three in the first place."

Gil thought about this. It was possible, of course. But why had they cut the hobbles on fifteen if they wanted only three? It just didn't make any sense. None of it did.

"What a terrible thing to happen to that poor horse that was killed," Jessica said, changing the subject. "I'm sure it was mine, the one I've been riding. I'm just sure it was."

"Oh, no, Jessica!" Lady Greenstreet said. "I think it was mine. Didn't you say it was brown, with a white spot on its forehead, Mr. Whitney?"

Gil shook his head. "I'm not sure whose it was. It may have been one of the packhorses."

"Aw, c'mon," Anson Leggitt said. "Who cares which one it was? A horse is a horse, for Pete's sake!"

"That's not *true*, Anson," Jessica protested icily. "The poor beasts lug us all over these mountains, and you talk about them like that!"

Gil finished his supper and left them to argue it out. He walked out into the night toward the partly completed horse corral. Halfway there, he heard footsteps being crunched in the gravel behind him. He turned. It was June.

"Can I walk with you?" she asked, stopping in some uncertainty as he turned. Then she added, "If you want to be alone, I'll go back. You don't have to say yes."

He smiled self-consciously. "I'm sorry, June. I should've asked if you wanted to come along. Of course you can."

"You seem anxious, Gil," she commented as they walked along slowly. "Or maybe frustrated. Are you in such a hurry to go back after the bear?"

He nodded. "It's the first real break we've had. I hate to let it slip away."

"You think the bear will come and go again before tomorrow?"

"It might. It might come and go two or three times, if it doesn't suspect something wrong. Likely, even a big bear will require several feedings to finish off a full-grown horse. I'm hoping that'll be the case anyway."

They stopped walking at the corral. What had been completed so far wasn't of the sturdiest construction Gil had ever seen, but it promised to serve the purpose. Aspen poles suspended in a three-rail span would hold adequately. With a little shoring up here and there, about ten more posts and twice as many poles as had already been cut, Gil figured the job should be finished. If they started early tomorrow, they could easily be finished by midafternoon. The horses would be allowed to graze along the river during the day, but would be penned each night and kept under guard. Gil knew that whoever ran them off the first time might not still be around, but he wasn't about to take a chance on that. For obvious reasons, he remained unable to convince himself that it had been nothing more than a simple matter of thievery.

"You want to finish the corral first, though?" June continued. "Before going after the bear?"

"Yes. Yes, I think I should do that."

"When will you go, then?"

He shrugged. "I'm hoping tomorrow, before dark."

"You'll be through with the corral by then?"

"I think so. With me here to help out, I think we can finish it in plenty of time. That part should be no problem."

"Will you be gone overnight?"

"There's a good chance of that, yes."

She seemed troubled by this. "You'll take Sir Robert and Sir Henry with you, of course."

Gil nodded. "It wouldn't be fair not to take them. It's their hunt, after all. But I know what you're thinking. We'll be leaving it mostly to you and Antonio to run things. And what if those horsethieves or whatever they were come back? That part *is* a problem, all right, and it worries me too."

June leaned against the corral fence. "That's not what worries me, Gil. I really don't think they'll come back. It's Anson and Jessica I'm concerned about."

Gil frowned. "Anson and Jessica?"

"They've been fighting again. Mostly when you've been gone—like today. They started shortly after you left and haven't really let up since. It puts a real strain on the rest of us, let me tell you."

Gil's frown became an impatient one. The thought galled him more than a little bit that he might now be plagued on top of everything else by petty bickering between two of the party members. "What on earth are they fighting about now?"

"You know Anson," June said. "He's never going to be happy that he was dragged along on this hunt. That's still it mainly, I guess. On the other hand, I have to give him credit for trying. At times he really has, you know. He worked hard on that corral today—when he wasn't quarreling with Jessica, at least—and he has even tried to help around camp. It's just that . . . well . . . just now he's so jealous he's half beside himself. He's—"

"Jealous?" Gil interrupted incredulously. "Jealous of what—who?"

June averted her eyes slightly. "You, Gil," she said in a very low voice. "He's jealous of you."

"Me! Oh, come on now—"

She met his gaze firmly this time. "Of course, you. Who else? Don't tell me you aren't aware of how Jessica has been looking and acting around you lately. She is very infatuated with you just now. Surely you know that."

Gil stared at her. Then he shook his head. "I think you and Anson are both seeing things, June. I mean—"

Her unwavering gaze stopped him in midsentence. "I don't think so, Gil," she said. "And don't worry. I'm not accusing *you* of being infatuated with her. . . . You aren't, are you? Well, anyway, I'm not accusing you. And I'm not even saying that Jessica fully realizes how she feels. I used the word 'infatuation' on purpose, believe me. But Anson couldn't care less about the difference between that and true love. He's simply jealous. What's more, I think he's decided that Jessica admires you mostly because you're so capable, here in your own environment. He sees himself as a sort of out-of-place fixture relegated strictly to the sidelines. I think he's become very insecure about it and would like to show someone that he can do a few things. He just hasn't figured out what that is yet, is all."

Gil almost laughed, but then the situation struck him as a bit more serious than that. Trouble was, he didn't know what to do about it. He had no idea whatsoever.

"Look," he finally said. "My main problems are still that of the camp and getting the bear for Sir Robert and Sir Henry. I haven't encouraged Jessica and I've tried not to aggravate Anson. Tomorrow we finish the corral and late tomorrow I plan to take the hunters out to see if we can't follow up with the only hopeful sign we've had yet of the bear. I wish I didn't have to dump so much responsibility on you, June, but I've got to. I just have no other choice."

She shrugged, then smiled reassuringly. "I can handle it, Gil. Really I can. Antonio and I . . . and Lady Greenstreet and Lady Gatlin, too. For sure, don't sell them short; they are very good with Anson, believe me. I only wanted you to know how things are; I didn't want to worry you. And I really don't believe those horsethieves will come back, either. We'll be all right, really we will."

He sighed. "I hope so. We'll likely be gone overnight and maybe longer this time. If the bear doesn't come back to its kill and we decide to track it, we could be gone until we either find it or lose the trail altogether. I won't be able to tell you when to expect us back."

"Don't worry about it, Gil," she said reassuringly. "Believe me, we *will* be all right."

For a moment he studied her. Then he shook his head and decided it was as good a time as any to change the subject to something more comfortable. Talk, after all, didn't mean much. Come tomorrow afternoon they would be going once again after the bear, and Gil would just have to hope that June knew what she was talking about. He wished he could be so confident that everything would indeed be all right.

5

The two men sat looking down on the site of the bear's kill of two nights before. They'd found it after Gil had come and gone, saw where he'd dismounted to investigate and where both he and the dog had left tracks, knew beyond a doubt it was him. They'd waited on through the night, then the following day, hoping for either the bear or Gil—or both—to return. They were well hidden within a stand of pine located atop a nearby bluff overlooking the river. It was perhaps an hour yet until sundown.

"I still don't like this," Dawson Riddle grumbled, not for the first time. "First we run them horses off, now here we are waitin' as much for Whitney as we are the bear. I don't like this kinda business, Cunningham. By God, I don't!"

Garst Cunningham gave him an icy stare. "Who in hell are you to like or dislike anything, Riddle? You were glad enough to have my support when we started, by damn—to accept a grubstake when you couldn't provide for yourself, to use my packhorses and equipment. You're sitting on a second chance to get the bear, which just everybody doesn't get. It's your chance to show both Whitney and those Englishmen up, and everybody else who's laughed at you because of it. And now you tell me you don't like it!"

Riddle looked away uncomfortably. "I just don't like runnin' people's horses off, then waitin' up here to do I dunno what to 'em if they show up. That's all."

"Who in hell said we're going to do anything to anybody?" Cunningham asked sharply. "Did I say that? Hell no, I didn't. We're just going to make sure they don't beat us to the bear, is all. We're making sure if the damn thing's seen, we see it first and get first shot at it. What's wrong with that, for chrissake?"

Dawson Riddle just shook his head. He wasn't sure. He sighed and leaned back, vowing silently to say no more about it.

Neither of them spoke for several minutes, until Cunningham said suddenly, "I can't figure that damned bear out. I thought sure it would come back to feed again last night or this morning early. Now I'm not so sure. Do you think it figured out we're here?"

Dawson shrugged. "Dunno. The old bastard's cagey as hell; he might come back and he might not."

"And Whitney," Cunningham went on. "He's bound to know his best bet is to do just what we're doing: Stake out the carcass and wait. I figured for sure he'd be back by now."

"Maybe he'll come yet."

The rancher thought about this. "Yeah, maybe," he finally said with a skeptical look. "Maybe."

They fell silent once again; half an hour passed; the afternoon shadows grew long as the sun fell behind the trees at their backs. Dawson wanted to get up and walk around; he was bored and had long since grown stiff from having sat around so much. Cunningham leaned back against a pine trunk and closed his eyes for a few moments' rest.

Dawson went back to check their saddle horses, tied about twenty-five yards away and out of sight from the river. Their packhorses had been left in the camp the two men had established two miles away.

Finding everything in order with the saddle horses, he strolled back toward Cunningham and the lookout post. The sun was behind the mountains now in the west. He found Cunningham snoring lightly. Retaking his spot nearby, Dawson settled in comfortably and resumed his watch of the scene below.

For almost five minutes he sat there, his rifle in his lap and his eyes wandering almost aimlessly here and there past the base of the rock bluff where the bear had made its cache. Thinking idly about this and that, he was only half alert when suddenly a magpie flew squawking from a large spruce tree growing near the base of the bluff. Curiously, Dawson straightened and fixed his gaze on the area around and below the tree, then beyond. Moments later, he spotted movement in some underbrush about seventy-five yards downriver from the tree. This time he jerked to attention.

It was something large he'd seen down there. Even in the rapidly fading light, he could tell that much. And then it emerged from the brush, and not only were his views about its size confirmed, he knew beyond doubt now what it was.

With a trembling hand, he reached over to shake the still doz-
ing Garst Cunningham awake. An instant later he caught sight,
out the corner of one eye, of three riders coming single file from
upriver. They were not far away at all.

6

Even over the sounds of the river flowing past, Gil heard but
did not see the magpie squawk and fly away. He pulled up and
turned to his two companions.

"What is it, Whitney?" Sir Robert asked, reining in.

"Didn't you hear that magpie squawk?"

"Why, no . . . I guess I didn't. Why?"

"Magpies are natural racket makers," Gil said, "but they don't
squawk like that unless startled. I figure something's up—there,
beyond those trees dead ahead."

The two Englishmen exchanged uncertain glances.

"It could be almost anything," Gil explained, "but it makes it
worth keeping an eye out. We're not far now from where I found
the dead horse."

They rode on, alert now, watching, listening. They reached the
trees Gil had pointed out, entering the stand cautiously. As they
came to the other side, Gil pulled up.

"Over there—the rock bluff. At its base is where Fleck found
the horse." He surveyed the scene thoughtfully, in some ways
wishing he'd brought the dog along this time. But once again he
had left the setter with June, feeling as before that the girl might
need the animal even more than he would. Still, he sort of
wished . . .

Suddenly something moved near the base of the rock bluff, and
Gil's thoughts locked on what his eyes were still trying to make
clear. Sir Robert must have seen it, too, for he said, "Whitney
. . . by Jove, Whitney! What is that? Do you see it? Henry, do
you?"

Gil held up a hand, motioning for quiet. They were yet two
hundred yards or more away, but that was not so far that the
sound of excited voices might not carry to discerning ears. He

peered intently, almost afraid to believe what he thought his eyes were telling him, wishing to God the light was better so he could tell for sure.

"Whitney," Sir Robert whispered, more excited than ever now. "Is it the bear? *Is* it?"

"I think so. At least I think it's *a* bear. But don't move. Just be still. I may be wrong, but I think it's got its nose in the air. It may be suspicious already." He looked around. Unfortunately there was only open ground between the stand of trees and the bluff. But was it possible they had already been detected? What little breeze there was blew lightly in their faces; he doubted that they could have been scented or heard. But the bear did seem to be acting inordinately suspicious. Was it simply being cautious? He wondered.

"If it is the bear," Sir Henry whispered, "how are we going to get up to it? There is no cover between here and there. No bloody way I can see to sneak up on it."

Sir Robert patted the butt of his rifle confidently. "I've taken longer shots than that with Old Bess here. I can again, if it comes down to it."

Gil shook his head at this. "Not a good idea this time, Sir Robert. Not when your target is a grizzly. Your chances of a killing shot at this range are slim, believe me."

Sir Robert accepted this grimly. "But what are we to do? Just sit here and let the beast get away?"

Gil shook his head once more. "Just wait a minute. Let's see what he does. You can never tell where he'll go from there."

"But it's getting dark," the Englishman protested. "We won't be *able* to see it much longer."

"Well, you're right about that," Gil conceded, "which is one reason I figure it unwise to risk a shot from here. A wounded grizzly running around in the dark is the last thing we want. On the other hand, the poor light might give us our best chance. Bears see poorly, and if that actually is Old Tuffy out there, it's a cinch he's come back to feed on the carcass. Once he starts that, he'll be about as distracted as he'll ever get. It might be we can get close enough to get off a good shot."   •

"You mean sneak up on him?"

"Sure. On foot, in the shadows along the river's bluffs. Our only chance, really."

"Then we should get on with it, shouldn't we? I mean, before it truly is too dark to see."

"Give him a minute more," Gil insisted stubbornly. "See if he's going to feed."

They watched nervously without dismounting their horses as the bear remained motionless beneath the rock bluff. This went on for almost two minutes. Then, finally, the animal stirred; it ambled slowly over to where Gil knew the carcass must still lie and, after some cuffing and pawing around, settled down to rip and tear at what remained of its kill.

Gil dismounted and pulled his rifle from its scabbard, motioning for his companions to follow suit. He then tied his horse to a nearby bush and began looking around for the best way to go. Seconds later, he had decided; all three men moved out at a crouch, going only a few measured steps at a time through the early evening shadows, their rifles held ready and their eyes seldom removed from the base of the rock bluff.

They had gone a laborious seventy-five yards, when suddenly the bear let out a just discernible little woof and threw up its head. Gil sank down and froze; instinctively his companions did the same. The light was poorer than ever now, and although each man presumed that the bear had detected their combined presence, it was impossible to tell for certain which way the animal was looking. Truth to tell, Gil would have sworn its attention was focused on the bluff above and somewhat downriver from them. But of course he really couldn't tell that. . . .

Sir Robert very slowly raised his rifle and bolted a shell into its firing chamber. "The beast is alerted, Whitney. No question about it. I'm going to shoot!"

Gil's eyes were fastened on the dark shape of the bear. The distance was still in excess of a hundred yards—not the very best of situations at all, with the light the way it was; but the Englishman's rifle was powered for long range and big animals, as was Sir Henry's, and Gil's own .50-95 Express was no slouch. It was very likely the best they were going to do.

"Okay," he finally said. "Sir Henry and I will back you up. Just aim for the heart and make your shot count. Say when you're ready."

The Englishman apparently couldn't steady his rifle to his satisfaction while kneeling, and thus dropped to a belly-flat position to try again. Both Gil and Sir Henry quickly followed suit, their rifles already cocked for firing.

"Ah, that's a bloody bit better," Sir Robert announced, his eye squinted and his finger firm and ready to tighten on the trigger. "I've got him square on—just where I want him, by Jo—"

He never finished his sentence. A shot rang out, but it was not his and it was neither of his companions'. Its echo reverberated up and down the river canyon and was interrupted only by the sound of a bullet ricocheting off rock somewhere up ahead. Three more shots resounded over the first in rapid succession, then another and another. Gil was so startled he took his eye off the bear the instant of the first shot. Instinctively, he had begun looking around for the shooter or shooters. He did not find them, and by the time he looked back for the bear it was gone. There was no sign of it anywhere.

Sir Robert and Sir Henry met Gil's look with expressions of pure astonishment and disbelief. "Who in bloody hell was that, Whitney?" Sir Robert finally asked. "By God, who did that to us?"

Gil's jaws were set so tightly with anger he almost couldn't speak. "I don't know. But they were shooting at the bear, not us. I think they were somewhere in the trees atop that bluff over there."

"They?" Sir Henry echoed. "You think there were more than one?"

"I'm sure of it. I heard reports from two different rifles, no question about it."

"And the bear?" Sir Robert wanted to know. "I saw him whirl and then he was gone. Do you think they hit him?"

"I sort of doubt it. The first shot ricocheted off rock; the others sounded wild, as if they knew the bear was getting away. My guess is they never touched him."

Sir Robert plainly found precious little solace in this. "And I didn't even get off a shot. I froze when I heard the other man's rifle report. I actually froze!"

"We all did," Gil told him. "There was no way any of us could have expected something like that." He paused thoughtfully. "I wonder if they knew we were here. I wonder if they opened up on purpose, just to keep us from getting the bear. . . . I wonder!"

Sir Robert's eyes became the thinnest of slits as he studied the bluff Gil had indicated. "Why would anybody do that, Whitney? *Who* would do it?"

Suddenly all three of them exchanged looks of realization.

Sir Henry, wide-eyed, said, "You think it's that Dawson Riddle bloke and your rancher friend—what's his name . . . Cunningham? You think it might be them?"

Gil didn't answer. He just looked at the now almost indiscernible stand of trees atop the bluff. A dark backdrop had all but hidden them now. A moon on its way to being full hung in the sky as if it had been painted there, but did not yet furnish much light. Gil wondered if whoever had done the shooting might still be there, or if they had long since taken their leave; he wondered who they were. Could it, by any stretch of the imagination, have been Dawson Riddle and Garst Cunningham up there? Could it indeed?

They camped overnight on the riverbank, and first thing next morning made their way atop the bluff. Sure enough, within the stand of pines Gil had pointed to the night before, they found plenty of sign of the shooters: Where two horses had stood tied for perhaps a night and a day; where two men had set up camp and waited and walked around and apparently waited some more; where half a dozen empty shells of two different calibers of rifle had been ejected and left after firing; where an apparently hasty evacuation of the place had been effected, probably very soon after the shooting had occurred.

They followed the two sets of horse tracks down to the river. A crossing had been made at a point nearly a quarter of a mile below where the bear had been seen and shot at. The tracks were temporarily lost there in the rocks. After only a halfhearted effort to relocate the trail on the other side of the stream, Gil suggested they go back and see if they could pick up any sign of the bear. In particular, he wanted to see if they could find some indication whether or not the animal had been hit.

They found plenty of sign. All around the rock bluff and the horse carcass were telltale paw prints with the proper toe marks missing; there was even scat. But look as they might they found no blood sign. They saw where the bear had whirled at the first shot, where it had dug its heels in to run, followed to where it, too, had crossed the river and had lumbered out on the other side. They could have followed it farther, except Gil remained intensely bothered by something else.

He just could not shake off his thoughts about those two men who had shot at the bear. He had lain awake most of the night thinking about them, connecting one event with another, thinking not only of the shooting incident but of the two riders who had watched the camp from the slope across the river and the stampede of the horse herd. And because these things did so seem to connect, no longer could he ignore or set aside any of it in favor of continuing the hunt. To him, now, one thing had to be settled before the other was pursued further. He wanted no more of what had happened last night.

"What is it, Whitney?" Sir Robert asked, seeing Gil's hesitancy. "You don't want to go on after the bear?"

"I'm not sure. I do know I don't much like trying to hunt grizzly with two men roaming around doing everything they can to interfere. I don't like not knowing what they're liable to try next, or when. And I certainly don't want to get killed because some fool wounded a grizzly while I was trying to sneak up to it on foot!"

Sir Robert eyed him. "You think now that those men might really be Dawson Riddle and Cunningham?"

Gil fingered the latigo on his saddle thoughtfully for a moment, then looked up. "I'm having a hard time thinking who else they might be."

"And you want to go after them? You want to find out for sure who they are?"

Gil nodded. "Yes. Yes, I suppose I do."

"And if we find them—what do we do then? What can we do?"

"I don't know," Gil said wearily. "But we'll think of something.

If we want to go on with the hunt, we'll have to think of something."

They returned to the point where the two riders had crossed the river. Upon making a much more intensive effort this time to do so, they finally located where the pair had come out on the other side, approximately two hundred yards downstream. The tracks led away from the river, in the direction of the mountains to the east.

Because an obvious effort had been made by the twosome not to leave a clear trail, the trackers did not make good time. It was almost noon by the time they had gone two miles, and it was half an hour later when they stumbled upon a long-abandoned trapper's cabin, half-hidden within a dense stand of fir and spruce. Its roof caved in perhaps years earlier by a heavy snowpack, the small structure looked to have achieved a sorry state of repair that rendered it well beyond further use. Gil, in fact, had not even known of its presence. But quite plainly the two men they were following had, for their tracks led directly to it, and against one wall a brush-covered lean-to had only recently been constructed. Out back, a half-fallen corral had been reinforced with brush and aspen poles, and inside its confines stood two horses, each of which nickered happily at the sight of the approaching riders and their mounts.

A quick survey did not indicate the presence of anyone else, however. Gil and the two Englishmen pulled up and exchanged cautious looks.

"Do you suppose they're hiding out somewhere, Whitney?" Sir Robert asked worriedly. "I mean, we could ride right into an ambush here, you know. That is what you call it, isn't it—an ambush?"

Gil nodded, but only said, "I don't think they'd do anything that extreme, Sir Robert. And I sure don't see any sign of them. . . . They must be gone."

After a few moments more of scanning the area, they decided to approach further. Indeed they found no one around. There were only the two horses, the lean-to, and a goodly amount of camp gear and supplies stashed beneath it to evidence that anyone had been there at all. But someone *had* been there and fairly recently. A now cold campfire had been doused apparently sometime that morning, and fresh boot tracks were found all around. Not far away lay the stake ropes where at least four horses had been staked out to graze overnight. Over by the corral lay two packsaddles and beside these rested a pair of feed bags, likely used to grain the horses inside the corral sometime earlier that morning. Two sets of fresh horse tracks led off to the north and disappeared crossing a pretty little clearing, through which, some seventy-five yards away, a small creek ran.

"They've come and gone," Gil told his companions. "And the way they've left the camp, I'm not sure they'll be back soon. My guess is they've gone off looking for the bear again. They probably watered and fed these horses before they left and they might even stay gone overnight. I'd sure as hell hate to have to wait around that long to catch them."

Sir Henry looked around. "Then what *do* we do? We haven't even learned for certain who they are yet."

They were standing next to the corral, and Gil was looking at the two horses inside. "Well, I wouldn't say that exactly. Do you see the brands on those horses? Look at the left hip on the sorrel . . . see what I'm talking about? That's Garst Cunningham's Rafter C, big as hell. Same thing on the bay. It's Cunningham and Riddle—I'd bet on it!"

"They want the bear and they'll do almost anything to keep us from getting it," Sir Robert concluded, albeit with a perplexed frown. "I guess I can understand the Riddle bloke feeling that way, Whitney. But why Cunningham? I thought you two were neighbors, that you were at least on civil terms."

"I did too," Gil said. "But I think I know what his problem is . . . I just didn't think it would go this far. And I guess it doesn't really matter now why they're doing it. The question is, what are *we* going to do about it?" He looked around thoughtfully.

Sir Robert shook his head. "There bloody well doesn't seem much we can do, unless we catch them and face them with it. And as you say, we could certainly waste a lot of valuable time by just sitting here waiting for them to show up."

Gil, still thoughtful, was back to eyeing the two horses inside the corral. "Maybe not," he said. "Maybe it doesn't have to be that way."

"What do you mean?"

"Think about what they tried to do to us. They ran our horses off and cost us a good two days rounding them back up and building fence to hold them. At that, three are apparently still running around somewhere and one has been lost for good to the bear. What if we turned the tables on them? What if we see how they like some of their own medicine?"

Sir Robert now was staring at the two horses also. "You mean turn these animals loose? But what good would that do? They are obviously only packhorses. How do we know Cunningham and Riddle would even bother to go looking for them?"

Gil walked over and hefted one of the packsaddles with one hand. Then he looked over at the cabin and the lean-to. "I think they might, under the right circumstances . . . say, if all of their gear and supplies were also missing." He mulled the idea over. "Look, I wouldn't ordinarily think of doing something like this, but Dawson and Cunningham have earned it, and we could sure use the time it might take them to chase those horses down."

Sir Robert looked over at Sir Henry, then back at Gil. "I'm still not sure I understand. What, exactly, are we going to do with their gear? Hide it? Carry it with us?"

"Neither," Gil said. "I think I've got something even better in mind. First, we catch and saddle the two horses. We'll load the gear on the packsaddles in a loose fashion, tie it on just well enough that it'll stay on for a ways but not too far, then turn the horses loose and maybe drive them over the hill to get them started." He paused, almost smiling. "After a while the packs will begin to shake or rub loose. Gear and supplies will fall off and scatter as the horses go. Cunningham and Riddle, missing their things as well as their horses, will almost surely follow the best tracks they can find, hoping to figure out what's happened. We'll mask our own tracks by dragging tree limbs or brush behind us until we're well beyond the camp. I figure it'll take Garst and Dawson at least a day or two not only to find their packhorses but to retrieve most of their gear. Meanwhile, we are back to hunting the bear."

Sir Henry lit his pipe, puffed heartily, then smiled. "Turn-about's fair play, eh, Whitney? Well, by Jove, I think I like it! I bloody well do! What's more, those men will not only waste some time catching their horses, they'll know—at least they should—that it's us who's done it. And they should know we're on to them because of it. Yes sir, that should make them think twice, too, before they pull any more shenanigans on us!"

Gil grinned. "Exactly."

"Okay," Sir Robert said. "I guess I'm with you. What do we do first?"

They went to work immediately, and twenty minutes later the two packhorses stood, packs loaded, tarp-covered and tied on loosely as Gil had suggested. Gil surveyed the situation, then told the other two men, "You fellows ride on back the way we came. Be sure and stay with the same trail. I'll head these horses on over the hill to the east, then backtrack till I catch up to you. When I get back here, I'll begin to drag some brush along behind me to wipe out our tracks. By the time Cunningham and Riddle figure out what's happened, it won't matter which way we went. They'll go on after their horses and we'll be free to go about our business."

He watched as the two Englishmen rode on off, then he removed the halters from the packhorses, slapped each on the rump in turn, and watched as they trotted off to the east. Then he mounted up and took off after them, driving them on until they were out of sight of the trapper's cabin. Half an hour later he overtook the two Englishmen; a couple of hours after that they were back on the river not far from where they first began tracking Cunningham and Riddle.

"We could probably try to pick up the bear's trail again," Gil told them, "but that's probably grown cold by now. Maybe we should go on back to camp and see how the women are doing. Tomorrow, we can start over again with the hunt."

It wasn't hard to get the two Englishmen to agree to this. No matter how hard he tried not to, each man had been worrying about those they had left behind. It would be good to see that all was well at the camp before going out again. They proceeded on back upriver without hesitation.

As it turned out, it was a good thing they went back. Along toward sundown they were met at the camp's outer perimeter by Lady Gatlin and Lady Greenstreet. Right behind them came Antonio, and it was plain immediately that something was wrong.

"It's Anson," Lady Gatlin told them, without waiting to be asked. "Last night . . , he slipped away without us knowing it. He took a horse and one of Sir Robert's rifles. He's disappeared. June and Jessica went after him this morning, but they've none of them come back yet."

"My God!" Sir Robert was the first to say. "Why on earth did Anson do that?"

"He and Jessica argued again," Lady Gatlin explained. "She made the mistake of telling him he wasn't much, just lying around and doing nothing. He wasn't much at all. She threw Mr. Whitney up to him again and I think he decided he'd show her. I think he went after the bear. I think that's how he's going to show Jessica he's something after all—by bringing in the bear!"

"Oh, Lord," Gil breathed, hardly able to believe what he was hearing. He looked at the Mexican boy. "Antonio, why in the world did you let June and Jessica go after him? Why didn't *you* go?"

The boy stood before them, trembling visibly. "I tried to stop them, Mister Gil. I told them I should go. I—I even saddled my horse and was ready to leave. But they wouldn't let me. They said I must stay with the ladies, here. They said they must go. They made me saddle their horses and get their rifles. They made me promise I would stay here."

Gil looked around, worry stirring frenziedly within him. The sun was riding depressingly low over the mountains to the west now; the day was all but done. He looked back at Antonio.

"Which way did they go?"

The boy pointed across the river. "That way, Mister Gil. They went that way, following Mister Anson's tracks. I don't know why they have not come back. . . . I don't know *why*."

Gil stared in the direction the boy had indicated. The mountains in the distance were bathed with deep hues of gold that would later turn pink, then purple, then fade away altogether as daylight finally was gone. Ordinarily his perception of such a view would have been one of beauty. But just now his thoughts were dark ones, and the mountains might just as well have gone black already.

CHAPTER 5

CLOSING IN

1

Sometimes various kinds of traps worked on grizzlies. Not many truly big bears were brought in this way because by and large this wary and sagacious lot had learned its lessons well, in cases of such trickery, long, long before. But now and then one succumbed, and because of this many were the times the approach was tried on the silver bear.

Two men, strictly motivated by the bounties being offered, made an intensive effort to trap the big grizzly in the fall of 1892. They were not slated to go down in history as famous men, and three years later few could remember anything much about them, except that their last names were Hicks and Larsen and they had come to San Juan country from somewhere upstate, near Gunnison.

For almost a month after coming to the area, they scouted around hoping to learn where the bear might likely be found. Everywhere they went they took with them a string of packhorses loaded with huge, forty-pound, steel-jawed bear traps, supplies, bedding, and guns. They were unquestionably well prepared. But they did not wish to waste time setting out traps until they had good reason to believe that the bear was in the vicinity. Thus they mostly rode from ranch to ranch, asking questions and hoping to hear what they wanted to know. They didn't have much luck, until one day they got word that the bear had only two days before been sighted near certain headwaters of the Little Navajo

River by some cowboys driving cattle down from the mountains toward winter range.

Posthaste, Hicks and Larsen made their way to Little Navajo country, and the cowboys who had reported the sighting. What they learned was, not only had the bear been seen as reported, but it was suspected as having ranged in the area since late summer. The cowboys ought to know, for as many as fifteen head of cattle were known to have been lost in the last two months alone to predators, and in over half those cases huge bear tracks had been left at the scene of the kill. And yes, three toes had been found missing from one front paw print, two from the other—Old Tuffy, beyond a doubt.

Hicks and Larsen ascended the Little Navajo to a point described to them as having been the scene of the recent sighting. Close by, they found a cowboy campsite, near which a pole corral had been constructed for the purpose of holding extra horses whenever cattle were being worked in the area. After some study, Hicks and Larsen decided they could use the corral to good advantage in their effort to trap the bear. A plan was thus formulated, which, they figured, was virtually foolproof if the bear would just show up and cooperate.

Recognizing the critical nature of this latter criterion, and fully aware that most if not all of the livestock that had been such easy pickings for the bear recently had now been driven to lower country, the two men went back downriver to the nearest ranch, purchased a thin old cow not expected to last the winter anyway, and led her back to the cowboy summer camp. Using eight feet of lead rope, they staked her in the center of the corral, removed one section of poles to serve as a gate opening, and proceeded to set steel traps all across the opening, connecting them with chains and tying each end to a sturdy fence post. These traps they carefully concealed by covering them with leaves and twigs. Then they set half a dozen more of the big traps in a circle around the cow, just far enough away from her stake that she could not reach one and accidently set it off. These, too, they concealed and interlinked to a heavy clog set several yards away.

So, convinced that the bear would have to trip at least one of *the traps if it attempted to get at the live bait inside the corral, the two trappers retired to a camp of their own a mile away.*

After a restless night's sleep they returned early next morning to see what had happened. The cow stood forlornly in the center of the corral where they had left her, unharmed. There were no bear tracks anywhere to be seen; no sign that the big grizzly had so much as come to investigate.

They watered and fed the cow and returned to their camp. The rest of the day and another night passed. Anxiously they returned the following morning to see what, if anything, had happened at the corral. This time something had. It just wasn't what they had expected.

The cow, they were surprised to learn, was dead, her stake rope had been bitten in two, and parts of her carcass had already been eaten away. Moreover, she was no longer in the center of the corral. She had been killed and bled there, then rather adroitly dragged between two of the traps that surrounded her to a point just inside the corral fence. Here, the carcass had been partly covered over with dirt and the only signs of the killer were tracks everywhere of an extraordinarily large bear. But no bear was to be seen; no traps had been sprung; and the astonished trappers were left with nothing to do but try to figure out how the feat had been accomplished.

The tracks told the story. Just outside the gate they found where the bear, having apparently scented the bait from some distance away, had approached, only to stop within inches of the first trap. Plainly the beast must have detected something, for straightaway it had gone away from the gate and circled the corral completely, at least twice. Finally it had crawled over the fence at a point well away from the gateway, breaking the top three poles in half with its weight as it went.

Inside, it had once again halted short of putting its foot in a trap, apparently investigated briefly those encircling the cow, then deftly stepped between two traps to kill what must by then have become a very frantic bovine. Having then dragged the dead animal across the corral to the fence, the bear had seemingly settled down to calmly eat its fill before scratching dirt over the carcass.

It then had gone back over the fence the way it had come and had gone no telling where from there.

Hicks and Larsen looked at one another, shook their heads in unison, then stubbornly brought out more traps and pulled those up that had originally encircled the cow. They left the carcass where it lay, encircling it now with concealed traps all the way to the fence on either end of a new line of traps. In no case was there more than a foot between one set of yawning, sixteen-inch, double-springed jaws and the next, and the entire system was again interlinked and tied off to fence posts. Even along the foot of the corral fence behind the carcass, they put traps. This time they were sure there was no way the bear could get to the remainder of its kill without sticking a paw in one of the traps. No way.

But just to make sure, they brought out a couple of set guns, tied them onto the fence, one on either end of the line of traps, and aimed them at a point directly above the cow's carcass. To the trigger of each gun they tied a silk line, and the two lines they then stretched in a V from the two guns to a point about five feet in front of the carcass. Here they drove a stake in the ground and very carefully tied off the two silk lines. Even if the bear did somehow get inside the trapline, it could not reach the dead cow without tripping one of the set guns. The silk lines, arranged at about two inches off the ground, were almost invisible, and it would be dark when the bear most likely would come. Surely now, there was no way the bear could get to the cow without setting off either a trap or a gun.

Once again the trappers returned to their camp to wait through another sleepless night. Two hours past sunup the following day, they were back at the corral. Indeed signs were clear that the bear had returned to its kill. But there was no bear, and once again not a single trap had been sprung. What's more, even the carcass now was gone! Hicks and Larsen looked at one another in astonishment, then began to piece together how once again their plans had been foiled.

The bear had approached in much the same manner as it had the night before, only this time it ignored the open gateway altogether. After circling the corral perhaps only once, it had crawled across the broken-down portion of fence it had used the first time, and moved suspiciously toward the carcass. But just as had been the case before, the tracks stopped short of the first trap. From trap to trap the bear had shuffled, to the fence one way and then the other way. Very carefully it had stepped between two of the traps and cautiously approached the dead cow. But just as it reached the silk line attached to the nearest of the set guns, it had stopped abruptly once more. Cautiously it had followed the line, without touching it, all the way to the fence and the set gun. It had then turned around, followed to where the line was tied to the stake in the ground and followed the second line to the fence and the second set gun.

Back through the trapline to its original fence crossing it had gone; outside it had crawled. Fresh paw prints went on a beeline for the area of fence beneath and within which the carcass still rested. Stiff hairs hung from cracks in the broken poles where the remains of the cow had been lifted over the traps set along the base of the fence, then dragged over the fence; signs on the ground showed plainly where the carcass had been dragged away, presumably to a place in the forest to be finished off by the bear.

Hicks and Larsen exchanged doleful looks, then began gathering up their traps. Two weeks later they were back in Gunnison country. They had a story to tell, but they did not—and knew now that they never would—possess the hide of the silver bear.

2

It was Jessica who had wanted personally to go after Anson. June at first had been in favor of sending Antonio. But something in the other girl's demeanor—the depth of her determination, mostly—had finally caused June to give in. Too, there was a serious question whether or not Antonio could do anything with Anson, even if he found him. June wasn't sure, now, why she herself had decided to accompany Jessica instead of letting Antonio at least do that, except that someone had to go and she hated to place the responsibility on the boy. She had not thought it would be that difficult or take that long to track Anson down. She just had not.

At first, it had seemed that she might be right in thinking this. The tracks of the single, shod horse were never difficult to follow. Anson had crossed the river directly, had entered the forest on the other side, then had wandered erratically southward using existing trails. Plainly he did not know where he was going or how to cover his tracks. And although June was by no means an accomplished tracker, she had a good head on her shoulders and she knew to take her time and not become careless. She had no intention of losing the trail in favor of a reckless forging ahead.

Trouble was, they had wandered around for most of the day now, climbing higher and higher in a country of scrub oak-covered hillsides, beautiful aspen groves, pretty mountain parks, and finally towering fir and spruce that stood so high and grew so close together that many times the position of the sun in the sky could not be determined, and still they had not come upon Anson. He was undoubtedly lost, but somehow as he led them all the while farther and farther from the river and the camp, he continued to elude them. Moreover, as the afternoon wore on, June and Jessica began to realize that they, too, might become lost. And even if they didn't, a point in time was soon to arrive at which they knew that too little daylight remained for them to make it back to camp before dark.

With sundown approaching, they dismounted atop a brushy little hill with a single, lightning-warped pine at its apex and a good view provided all around. As Fleck trotted up and flopped down beneath the tree, tongue out and panting, June stood looking forlornly back the way they had come, generally to the north and somewhat west.

"It's all my fault," Jessica bemoaned from nearby. "I drove Anson to this. I really did."

June looked over at her. Off and on all day Jessica had been saying this, and clearly her distress was sincere. But it did little good to go on saying it, and June had long since grown tired of having to listen. Nonetheless, she sighed patiently. "The problem now is, we didn't bring any bedrolls. Only a few biscuits, some jerky, and our jackets in case it rains. Whether we find Anson now or not, we're going to have to spend the night up here, and it may not be a very comfortable experience for either of us."

"How far is it back to camp?" Jessica asked, trying to follow June's gaze.

"Look for yourself," June told her. "That's Squaretop over there. I figure almost due north and no less than eight or ten miles away. Down there—that's the river, five miles from here at least. We're lucky we can even see it. It's the first time all day we've been where we could."

Jessica continued to stare. "And it's taken us all day to get here? My God, I feel like I've ridden fifty miles at least! My legs are so raw I'm not sure I can walk, much less get back on that horse. . . . Oh, June, what have I gotten us into?"

June gave her a sympathetic look. "Maybe nothing all that bad," she said softly. "We just have to keep our heads and not panic, that's all. Look, I've been out like this before—well, maybe not quite like this—but out, anyway. We mustn't go on after dark or we really will get lost. We'll have to make camp. It'll be chilly toward morning, but not so cold that we'll freeze, and we can use our saddle blankets and build a fire to keep warm. We'll make it, don't worry. We even have a little bit left to eat. And tomorrow, if we don't find Anson pretty quick, we'll get our bearings and head back. I'm sure we can refind the river, and when we do that we'll eventually find camp. Maybe Gil and the others will be back by then and they can hunt for Anson."

"But that's just it," Jessica said, slightly horrified. "Anson is up here alone, and he's probably even less able to take care of himself than we are. I really am afraid for him, June. Really I am."

"He's a grown man, Jessica. And he's the one who took off, remember? If we don't find him with what's left of today or early tomorrow, he'll just have to make do for himself until Gil and the others can take up the search. You and I simply didn't come prepared to stay up here. Anson at least did make off with a bedroll, plenty of food, and one of Sir Robert's best rifles."

Jessica didn't look greatly comforted, but she did seem too tired to argue. She looked around. "Where will we camp? Here? June . . . are you listening to me?"

June, caught momentarily staring at the ground, looked quickly up. "No," she said, almost too hurriedly. "I mean, we won't camp here. I . . . think back down the hill a ways instead . . . maybe at the bottom of that last little canyon we crossed. There's a creek there, and I'm sure there'll be more protection there from the cold tonight." Continuing to force her eyes away from what she had just seen on the ground, she looked back to the east. She tried hard to sound reassuring as she added, "Don't worry. Anson's tracks go off that way. It won't take us long to relocate them tomorrow."

"Well, I hope not," Jessica said, turning toward her horse. "I only hope we can find him before we have to go back . . . before something terrible happens to him. . . ."

June could only sigh and nod her head. If someone had told her a month ago she would wind up in a situation like this, she would have laughed until there were tears. Today, she was afraid there might merely be the tears. Not only was Jessica right to be worried, she hardly knew the half of it.

As they made their way down the trail a few minutes later, June decided, at least for now, not to tell her about the unbelievably large and freshly made bear track she had just seen on the trail atop the hill.

3

Of all the horses released by Cunningham and Riddle at the river camp those few nights before, Gil had failed to recapture only four. Three had been among those purchased in town by the Englishmen, and of these, one had of course been killed by the bear; the other two had simply escaped and were now wandering loose in the hills to the south. The fourth horse had come from among Gil's own ranch stock, a gray gelding that had been following along in the company of the one that had been killed at the time the bear had jumped it.

Few things will strike fear in a horse like the sight or smell of a bear, especially at night, and the gray was no exception to this. Already skittish at having been separated from their companions in the dark, the two horses had been wandering along the river when the bear had suddenly come rushing out of the trees to down the one in the lead. Frantically the gray had whirled to run. Neither slowing down nor looking back until the river was put well behind, it soon found itself completely alone and without the comfort of the other horses to settle its nerves.

Anxiously the horse had trotted along this trail and that, nickering frightened but futile calls to its lost companions. The darkened forest responded with eerie silence and inky emptiness. The horse remained starkly alone.

For a while the animal wandered mostly west and somewhat south of where it had left the river. Later it turned north. It trotted along, bolting now and then at the night shadows, running for a ways, slowing down again, trotting, dancing, head held high, nervous, frightened.

The sun rose. The horse reached Sheep Cabin Creek, followed its willow-infested course upstream, came to the Little Blanco. Daylight lessened the animal's anxiety. Birds chirped; cattle grazed the slopes nearby; deer raised their heads to watch the horse in mild curiosity, then went back to their grazing. The gray, too, stopped to graze. No longer so frightened, it began to move about somewhat aimlessly. It kept this up the rest of the day, that night, and the next day, although it stayed close to the Little Blanco, for a source of water was always assured there. Still it was restless. Farther and farther it worked its way upstream, vaguely looking for the other horses.

Finally, having despaired of finding others of its kind, its instinct to return home, to the horse pasture at Gil's ranch in Echo Canyon, turned it west again. From there on, even as it grazed, the animal did not waver from its course.

Shortly after breakfast, the third morning the horse had been on its own, Buck Blaine went up the hill behind the house to cut some firewood. Half an hour later he heard a horse whinny from somewhere in the vicinity of the corrals. From yet farther away, probably the horse pasture, came an answering neigh. Buck's first thought was that a rider was approaching the house, but the corrals and the road were out of sight from where he worked, so he decided to go on down the hill to see what was what.

He found the gray standing outside the corrals by the barn, nickering and prancing excitedly back and forth. Half a dozen other horses were coming at a canter from well out in the horse pasture, obviously curious and bent on investigating the new-comer. Buck recognized the gray immediately as one of the horses Gil and the hunting party had taken with them, and puzzlement struck him as he saw the remains of its hobbles still dangling from a front foot. He went inside the barn and reappeared with a rope halter. Catching the gray easily, he saw that it was unharmed but was quite nervous and glad to be home. He removed what was left of the hobbles, and for the first time realized that they had been *cut*, not broken!

Worriedly he looked up. He had no way of knowing what cir-cumstances had caused the horse to be cut loose, but the possi-bility of something having gone wrong at the hunters' camp was too great to ignore. He debated what he should do.

He knew where on the Blanco River Gil had said they would make camp; he knew he could be there in less than a day's time if he so chose. Still, he was undecided. Should he leave the ranch unattended and go, or not?

He led the horse inside the main corral and over to a trough that had been placed against an outer wall of the barn. Then he went back inside the barn and returned with a measure of grain, which he emptied into the trough. He stood thoughtfully by as the horse fed. A few moments later the horses from the horse pas-ture came trooping through an open gate into the corral. Buck, still thoughtful, watched as the entire bunch crowded around the newcomer and the trough, and after a moment he walked slowly across the corral and closed the gate behind them.

His mind made up now, he returned to the barn, moments later reappearing with bridle and saddle in hand. He might have to push it a bit, but he was pretty sure he could yet gather up his rifle and gear at the house and be on the Blanco by nightfall.

4

If Anson Leggitt was to somehow weather his second night alone in the hills, he would do it at best in utter misery. He was lost, he was cold, and he was frightened. And what he himself had so stubbornly started in steamy anger the night before, he would now have ended meekly any way he could. But that was the problem: He *couldn't* end it, because he hadn't the slightest idea how to go about doing so.

Mainly, he didn't know where he was. All day he had ridden around, ostensibly doing what he'd vowed to himself he would do —trying to find the bear. At first, he was so taken with the idea, so determined to show Jessica that he was just as much a man as Gil Whitney or any other, that he hadn't thought a lot about finding his way back to camp or even having to. That first night had not been so bad; it was only a part of a night, after all, and his determination was still strong. Later, as the day arrived and then wore along and his fervor started to wear thin, it began to dawn on him that he might be lost. By an hour before sundown, the fact had not only dawned, it had become coldly sobering.

Wandering around alone in full daylight had been one thing; the prospect of surviving the coming night was distinctly another. At least to Anson Leggitt it was . . . a man who knew almost nothing of even the most basic skills required to accomplish what he had set out to do.

It was nothing he shouldn't have known already, even last night following his argument with Jessica. But such rational thought had eluded him then. Beside himself with anger, he had stormed away from the camp to tramp alone for nearly an hour along the darkened riverbank. He had not calmed down as he walked. And it came to him that he must do something—anything at all—to show Jessica. Thus with anger, frustration, and jealousy sufficiently clouding his judgment, he had thought of the bear. That was how he would show Jessica, how he would show them all. He would go himself to bring in the bear.

He knew it would not be easy, but at that point he had been so seething with angry determination he didn't care. He would do it no matter what. Even if they caught him stealing away, he would not be stopped. He would go anyway.

Still, it had suited his purpose to leave without the others knowing. In the morning they would know, and that would be soon enough. He would need a horse, rifle, ammunition, food, and bedroll. He would have to work it out so that they did not know when he left. Stalking along the riverbank on his way back to camp, he had decided how it could be done. He would volunteer to sleep near the horse corral, to take the responsibility for guarding it through the night. He would order Antonio to sleep near the camp. Anson would carry his bedroll, saddle, and bridle to the spot where he proposed to make his bed. When the others were asleep, he would steal back, take one of Sir Robert's extra rifles, ammunition, and food as needed. He knew where all of these things were and he was sure he could do it. His only real problems were the Mexican boy—who might wake up—and the dog. The dog might bark or growl and wake them all. But the boy usually slept soundly and Anson had long since made friends of Gil Whitney's big white-and-black setter; he did not really expect trouble there. If he could just catch his horse from among the horse herd in the corral, if he could just manage to do all he must do without waking the camp, then he was sure he could pull it off.

And pull it off he had. Somehow, two hours past midnight, he had. And now he wished to God he had not. What a ridiculously stupid stunt it had been.

He wasn't going to find the bear—he knew that now. He had found only rough country and rough going, where the trees were many times too tall for him to see the sun and get his bearings much of the time, where most landmarks—because he did not know them—became more confusing than helpful, and where even knowing which side of the trees moss grew on did him little good, for he hardly knew which direction he needed to go in to get back to camp anyway.

In his hurry to get away, he had become lost even before the sun came up. He wasn't sure which direction he had been riding during those dark early-morning hours, and thus had no idea which direction he should ride to go back. He had confused south for east, then east for south, then south again for east, all before he realized that the sun was suddenly now coming up in the north, and of course that could not be!

So he had ridden on, climbing at times on slopes so gradual he did not realize that climbing was what he was doing, unable to see the river and too confused, amazingly, to realize that he must follow the canyons downhill, not uphill, to reach it. He had gone on until dark and was forced to make camp. He had realized then that he had no matches, and because he knew no other way to make a fire, he could not even do that. He did not know how to hobble his horse and thus was forced to tie it by its bridle reins to a nearby bush. He struggled almost as much to get the saddle off as he had struggled the night before to get it on. What he had brought to eat was all cold food—biscuits, jerky, canned fruit. He had nothing to cook and no way to cook it. He had no canteen and did not know how to return to the last creek he had drank from, even though he knew it was not far back on the trail. The dark frightened him, and he realized too, now, that he wasn't even sure how to load and fire the rifle he had brought with him. He thought he did, thought he had loaded it properly—but what if he had to shoot to protect himself? Assuming it fired, could he even hit anything?

What if he did indeed stumble upon the bear? Or *any* bear? Or a mountain lion, or whatever other kind of creature might lurk out there that might harm him?

He sat trembling in the darkness, cursing himself, wondering if anyone had—or would!—come after him. He heard all sorts of night sounds. He gazed up into the sky, saw stars everywhere, and a moon that had almost grown full. At least there were no clouds; there was some light.

An owl hooted, his horse stamped a foot, snorted. It was comforting to know at least that the horse was nearby.

Finally exhaustion claimed Anson. He crawled inside his bedroll and tried to get to sleep. Still he lay awake for maybe an hour before his heavy eyelids just would not stay open any longer. His weariness too much for him, he fell into a deep slumber.

When next he awoke, the sun's glare was in his face. He moaned, sat upright, then looked around with a start. It was broad daylight; the sun had been up at least two hours. Anson rubbed the sleep from his eyes and sighed. At least he had slept; nothing had happened to him. For the first time in his life a simple thing or two like that caused relief to wash over him. Daylight made things seem so much better, certainly not as bleak as last night.

Then he realized he had been too quick to judge his good fortune. He caught himself staring at the bush where he had tied his horse. The bush was of course still there and he was positive it was the right one. *But there was no horse!*

Alarmed, he looked all around. He leaped to his feet, searched for his boots, then sat back down to pull them on. Once again he came to his feet. Forgetting all about his rifle, he went charging over to the bush. Sure enough, there were tracks all over where the horse had been, dung heaps, a large wet spot where it had urinated. Anson stared at the bush. He could have sworn he had tied the reins tightly . . . and sure enough, he had. They had been broken, for their knotted ends and about half their length still dangled from the limb where he had tied them. Now why had the horse pulled loose? The animal was as gentle as any the hunting party had brought with them—Gil Whitney had assured Anson of that. He had also assured him the animal would stand tied; all of the horses would.

But still it was gone. Its tracks led away at a lunging run, on down the trail. But Anson was too distraught, his eye too untrained, to figure even this out.

Not knowing what to do, dejected, he went back to his bedroll and flopped down on the ground. He just sat there. What *was* he going to do? He couldn't walk out of here, could he? Well, maybe he could . . . but which way to go? What if he went the wrong way? What if he walked until his feet were blistered and he still could not find his way back? What if something that could run faster than he could attacked him? Dear God. . . .

He was still sitting there half an hour later, mumbling to himself, when June and Jessica rode up and found him. And he was rendered almost speechless shortly thereafter when June showed him a set of enormous bear tracks made during the night, which left little doubt as to what had caused the horse to break its reins and run away. Worse yet, the tracks were most clearly made within six feet of Anson's bedroll.

5

Late the day before, Garst Cunningham and Dawson Riddle had returned to their camp at the trapper's cabin. They came in time to discover what had happened but much too late to do anything about it before nightfall.

Cunningham had been furious. "It was Whitney—it had to be. And a damned sorry thing it is, too: For someone to take not only a man's pack animals, but to load up and steal his gear right along with them!"

Dawson, too, had at first believed that Gil Whitney and his friends had not only discovered but had stolen the two horses, supplies, and gear. But he was at least a little less indignant in his reaction to it. After all, hadn't he and Cunningham run the hunting party's horses off just three nights ago? Was turnabout not fair play, in such cases?

"The thing about it is," he told the other man calmly, "Whitney and them two Englishmen must've somehow trailed us here from the river. All they had to do was read the brands on them two packhorses to know they're your animals. Whitney'll know it's me and you up here lookin' for the bear, and he's probably put two and two together about what's been happenin' by now, too."

Cunningham turned to glare at him. "So? That in no way excuses—"

Riddle didn't let him finish. "Don't have to be excused. The point is, it's no worse than what we did. So how in hell can we go callin' on that huntin' party to get our stuff back without havin' to face up to our own tricks? Assumin', of course, they actually did take the horses and things with 'em. . . ."

"What do you mean by that?" Cunningham's eyes narrowed. "What do you mean 'assumin''?"

"It's the tracks." Dawson pointed around loosely at the ground. "They don't read right. I see three sets of hoofprints—I figure Whitney and the Englishmen. Two other sets come from inside the corral and are our pack animals. Three sets take off to the east, but only one of those is from Whitney's group, and that one comes back alone. The other two are those that come from the corral. They *don't* come back. Two more go I don't know where because someone's obviously scratched 'em out with some brush or something. Now, I don't know about you, but it makes me think a bit. Damned if it don't!"

"It makes you think what, exactly?"

"Well, it makes me think maybe they didn't actually take the horses. Maybe they did something else with 'em entirely."

"Like what? Say *what*, man!"

"Maybe they run 'em off. Just like we did their horses."

Cunningham stared. "Packs and gear and all? You really think that? Good grief, why?"

Again Riddle shrugged. "Same reason we did it to them, I reckon. To keep us busy huntin' our horses and stuff—which we'll have to do, all right—while they go after the bear. That and let us know they're on to us. It'd have to be that, too, of course."

For a few seconds it seemed as if Cunningham still did not believe. But then his expression changed. He shook his head and looked off into the dusky forest to the east. Belief seemed to flood over him as he breathed a very heavy, "Well, I'll be damned."

Early next morning a more detailed study of the tracks seemed to confirm Dawson's speculations. Where Whitney and the two Englishmen—if that was indeed who they were—had gone they could not tell, but half an hour from camp Cunningham and Riddle found themselves following only two sets of hoofprints—those of their own packhorses. There seemed precious little they could do but follow them on, which they proceeded unhesitatingly to do.

After a while they came upon a portion of one of the packs spilled alongside the trail. A canvas sack with about half of their cooking utensils lay within five yards of a small, partly spilled bag of flour. On up the trail they found a length of rope tangled in some brush, and the rest of their cooking utensils. Strewn along the trail for the next hundred yards or so were additional items— everything from food to extra ammunition to an axe—and finally another piece of rope and the tarp used to cover the second pack. Some kind of animal—probably a badger or coyote—had already been at the food and much of it was ruined. A little ways farther and they found the balance of the second pack. This, too, had been rummaged through by animals.

"They did it on purpose," Garst Cunningham declared. "They tied those packs so they wouldn't stay. They actually *wanted* us to find our stuff scattered all over like this!"

Dawson didn't say anything; he just stood and marveled.

"We can't carry all of this stuff with us," Cunningham went on, with a grim look back down the trail. "We'll have to gather it up as best we can and stash it someplace. Then we'll have to go on after the horses—Whitney's fixed us so we don't have any other choice, damn him!"

A while later they had everything they couldn't carry in their saddlebags or bedrolls—which was considerable—wrapped inside the tarps, which they then lashed tightly together. Finding a place nearby among some rocks in which to stash the gear, they then mounted back up to resume the search for the missing horses.

Along about noon they came upon a small meadow, along one side of which grew a magnificent stand of aspen. Near the aspens' edge, a small stream, running lengthwise with the meadow, had been dammed by beaver, and was thus swollen into a fair-sized pond. As they entered the clearing, Cunningham and Riddle heard more than one beaver tail slap water, and they saw at least one of the big, flat-tailed rodents slip into the water and disappear.

The trail they were following wound now through tall grass, and it soon became clear that the missing packhorses had paused here, probably sometime prior to sunup, to graze. Now, however, they were nowhere to be seen.

The problem thus became one of finding where the horses had left the clearing. The tall grass made tracking difficult, and eventually the two men were forced to split up and circle the meadow in an attempt to locate the horses' exit route. After about fifteen minutes of this, Dawson Riddle finally found the way in which at least one of them had gone, just above the beaver pond among the aspen. Dawson had been making his way around and over trees cut and felled by the beaver, when suddenly he saw tracks leaving the clearing. They had been made by a single horse and the animal appeared to have been going in a hurry.

Puzzled, Dawson called across the clearing to Cunningham, then continued to look. About twenty yards away he found a second set of shod hoofprints—the other packhorse, he was sure. It, too, had gone at ground-gaining strides, generally in the same direction as the first horse. As best Dawson could tell, the two animals had been grazing along separately when something must have startled them and caused them to cross the creek and flee.

A few moments later Cunningham rode up to join him. They had pondered the situation only briefly when, but a short distance away, they discovered the bear track. It was the print of a hind paw, was easily as fresh as the horse tracks, and was much too large to be that of any ordinary bear. To men who knew about such things, there was little doubt it had been made by a grizzly. And although a distinct front paw print could not immediately be found for certain confirmation of the bear's identity, there was also little doubt that the animal was at least large enough to be the great silver marauder the two men wanted so badly to bring in.

Because of this, they quickly forsook the horse tracks and began following those of the bear.

6

When Gil and his companions had arrived back at the river camp late the day before, and learned what had happened there, they realized that it was much too late in the day to effectively do any tracking of Anson Leggitt and the two missing girls. They had no choice but to wait the night through before taking to the trail, which of course they would do first thing next morning.

Naturally, Gil wasn't very happy about this. He was flatly disconsolate, in fact, at just the thought of June and Jessica having to spend the night alone in the hills—which, if they didn't come in soon, was exactly what they were going to have to do. Of course, even if they did stay out, logic told Gil that the girls would probably be all right. They hadn't taken bedrolls with them, nor much food. But they had carried their rifles, were riding gentle horses, and had at least had the presence of mind to take the dog. Aside from the discomforts they would likely endure, they should be able to at least make do. June would see to that. . . .

Nonetheless, Gil was not much comforted. There were dangers, likely or unlikely, with which perhaps even June could not cope, and Gil could not help worrying because of this. Worse, he didn't even want to think what might happen to Anson, perhaps still wandering around out there alone and probably lost. He hardly wanted to think of any of it.

On top of all else, he didn't like the idea of going out tomorrow and leaving Lady Gatlin and Lady Greenstreet alone in camp with only Antonio to take care of them. Especially he didn't want to leave them alone overnight, should that become necessary. He was inclined to try to convince one of the Englishmen, probably Sir Henry, to stay behind. But it was no easy business, tracking—especially when trailing someone who might be lost. And with only Gil and Sir Robert to do the searching, their problems might become intolerably compounded if the trails left by Anson and the two girls had somewhere along the way begun to diverge. Such a possibility was all too likely and could very well dictate that the trackers split up in order to find all parties. The trouble with this was, sending Sir Robert off on his own might do no more than get him lost also, and Gil didn't need that to add to his other troubles. He thought of taking Antonio along, but then he would be leaving only Sir Henry in charge of the camp, and he really didn't want that, either.

Unfortunately, neither tenderfeet nor young boys, willing as they might be, were the kind of help Gil needed now. Maybe it wouldn't matter that much in the long run, but he sure would feel better if he had someone else along who knew his way around; someone who knew the country and could track at least as well as Gil could. God, how much better that would make him feel. . . .

And so it was that one thing finally went right for Gil that day, when a few minutes later, just before dark, a lone rider appeared coming up the river . . . and that rider turned out to be Buck.

7

June and Jessica had come upon the bear tracks again about a quarter of a mile past the top of the hill. They had risen at sunup, had eaten sparingly, and had then broken camp with the immediate resumption of their search for Anson in mind. Back atop the hill, they had easily relocated his tracks. The trail had led them then into a dark little canyon overgrown with trees, where they almost immediately came upon the great paw prints, entering the trail. This time, June found the fact impossible to hide from Jessica.

The dog, bounding along ahead of them, was first to discover the sign. It ran back and forth in great agitation, sniffing at the trail as it went. The tracks were so distinct they almost leaped up at the two girls as they rode up to see what had so excited the dog.

The bear had come onto the trail from off to one side and had begun following its course straightaway. Its tracks were not only quite fresh but had obviously been made since those of Anson's horse, which had probably gone the same way late the day before.

Jessica's eyes grew round as she viewed the tracks. "My God, June—look how huge they are!"

June, having already dismounted, bent to inspect the trail more carefully. The paw prints were indeed large, and they were so very fresh that June actually imagined she could smell the heavy scent of the beast still in the air. No question the dog could, for already it was fifty yards down the trail, still sniffing excitedly and whining. The bear must have come along during the night or early-morning hours, perhaps had detected the scent of Anson's horse, then quite probably had taken to the trail after it.

Alarmed, June quickly remounted. "Come on, Jessica. No more poking around for us. I don't like the looks of this at all."

The other girl started to say something, but before she could, June had spurred her horse into a canter and was off down the trail following the dog. Jessica, though somewhat frightened by both the sudden sense of urgency and the pace, could do little else but follow.

Half a mile farther and they came upon Anson, the dog racing up to him first, the two girls coming right behind. June was no more surprised at how happy and relieved the young man was to see them than she was at how ashen his face became when she showed him the bear tracks that had been made so frightfully close to his bedroll.

For a while they just stood around and talked, Anson readily admitting what a fool he had been and the girls agreeing, silently, with his every word.

Strangely, however, Jessica did not choose to berate or belittle him. Instead, she showed only concern. Too, she was apologetic for her own part in the affair, and she evidenced a degree of tenderness toward the young man that took June completely by surprise.

It must have surprised Anson also, for he hardly seemed to know how to respond to it.

"Well, the main thing now," June finally told them, "is for us to figure out how we're going to get back to camp. Did you look for your horse at all, Anson? Are you sure he's run completely off?"

Anson looked at her as if she were crazy. "Wouldn't you? If that monster of a bear came after you, wouldn't you run completely off?"

She smiled. He was right about that, of course. The horse probably had run all the way to the river without stopping, and chances were, if they ever saw it again, it would not be before they themselves were back in camp.

"Okay," she said. "There's probably no use us even trying to find the horse. We'll just have to head back without it."

Anson, who hardly seemed to hear, just shook his head. "To think, the thing walked right past me. Why didn't it kill me? Do you think it didn't know I was here?"

June sighed. "That's possible, Anson. It may have been so intent on getting to your horse it never noticed you. But that doesn't mean it would have attacked you even if it knew you were there. Grizzlies have forever been accused of making unprovoked attacks on man, but I don't believe I've ever heard tell of Old Tuffy attacking anyone who didn't attack him first. Who knows, lying there sound asleep in your bedroll might possibly have been the safest thing you could have been doing."

Anson didn't look very convinced, but he did look thankful. For whatever the reason, he knew how lucky he probably was just to be alive.

"About heading back for camp?" Jessica asked, a little pale herself. "What do we do—without Anson's horse, I mean?"

"Well, the simplest thing is for Anson to ride your horse. Since you and I are lighter, we'll ride double on mine. He's gentle enough, I'm sure."

"And which way do we go?"

This time, June was less certain. She glanced back up the trail, then down it. She looked at her shadow, gauging both the time of day and the direction, then she looked back at Jessica thoughtfully.

"I'm not sure," she said. "We could go back the way we came, try to follow our own backtrail of yesterday. But that involved so much wandering back and forth and around in circles, I'm not sure it would be the best way. I think perhaps a faster way would be to follow this trail until it tops out someplace where we can see far enough to get our bearings, then head northwest toward the river. The main thing is to avoid any more of these canyons. No matter how well you think you know your directions when you enter one, it's all too easy to get turned around as you go and wind up heading another direction altogether. For sure, we don't want to wind up on the Little Navajo or some such place instead of the Blanco. It might take days to find our way back if that happens."

"I don't care how we do it," Anson said. "I just want to get back."

June looked at Jessica, only to be met with a shrug. "Don't ask me, June. I have never been so lost in all of my life. Whatever you say, we'll do, but I'm afraid that's about all the help either of us can be. I'm sorry, but it's entirely up to you. You alone must decide."

Heaving a little sigh, June acknowledged to herself that of course the other girl was right. It was fully up to her to get them back. Between the two of them, Anson and Jessica were still too lost and too inexperienced to do anything but follow. But then she told herself: Things could be worse. She glanced skyward, noting that not a cloud was to be seen. It promised to be a pretty day, was yet early, and there was plenty of time for them to reach the river if they could just settle on a reasonably direct way of getting there.

Once again she settled her gaze on the down part of the trail.

After a few moments of thought, she turned back to her companions. "Okay. We'll try the trail that way. Anson, we need to roll your bedding up and find a place to stash your saddle till someone can come back for it. And we'll have to get a move on, too. It'll be all we can do to make camp before dark as it is." She paused as Anson seemed slow to respond. "Well, come on! Surely you don't want to spend another night out with that bear wandering around your camp, do you? Well, *do* you?"

From the way the young man turned quickly to the tasks at hand, it was obvious that of course he did not.

8

Hours later but only a few miles away, Dawson Riddle stood wearily beside his horse, his eyes on the trail before him. Garst Cunningham stood not far away, in much the same pose. Neither man was very happy at the moment.

About an hour earlier they had come to a point where the bear had suddenly and inexplicably abandoned the trail. For whatever reason, the big animal had stopped, then turned aside to enter a sprawling hillside stand of scrub oak. The brush, almost too thick for a rider to penetrate, had made further tracking all but impossible; and try as they might Riddle and Cunningham had been unable to find where the bear had come out on the other side. Likewise, neither man was about to go plunging blindly into the thicket looking to see if the beast was still in there. Even the outside chance of stumbling onto the hairy outlaw in such close quarters was too frightening to contemplate.

So, they'd hung around for a while, waiting to see if the bear actually had concealed itself on the hillside and was yet up there, perhaps watching them. They had even thrown a few rocks into the brush and whistled and hooted, hoping to stir the animal to come rushing out and be seen. But all this had accomplished was to disturb a couple of noisy magpies, an equally noisy jay, and perhaps a few chipmunks. Nothing else had moved. The bear simply was nowhere to be seen.

Thus, they now had concluded that they had little left to do but give up for the time being on the bear and return their attention to the trail of their missing packhorses—which, as luck would have it, the bear had been quite diligently following right up to the time it had so mysteriously taken to the brush. Wearily, they mounted back up, knowing that relocating the tracks of the horses would be no problem; the wayward animals had come back together shortly after having bolted the clearing of the beaver pond and had stayed that way ever since. They were traveling a well-worn trail, and the two men did not expect to find the tracking of them difficult.

Nevertheless, they had gone for but a short distance when something happened that neither man was sure how to explain. A third set of hoofprints suddenly entered the trail, and they were those of a shod horse that seemed to have joined with rather than have come to follow the other two. At this point, Cunningham and Riddle came to a halt and began trying to decide what, if anything, this new development meant to them.

"I figure the horse is running loose, just like our two," Cunningham concluded after studying the tracks at some length. "No telling where it came from or why it's loose, but I'm sure that's the case."

Dawson squinted at him. "What makes you sure? How can you tell, for instance, that it don't have a rider?"

"I can't . . . absolutely. But look at the way the tracks tell it. The first two horses stop and wait for the third to catch up. They mill around quite a bit, probably getting acquainted. After that, all three head on down the trail in no big hurry. See here . . . see what I'm talking about? Not the way it would happen if a rider showed himself to them. I know those two jugheads of mine; faced with a rider, their first instinct would've been to run, not stop and wait. Do you see what I mean?"

Dawson nodded slowly. "I reckon I see that, all right. But what's it doin' here? Where'd it come from?"

Cunningham shrugged. "I figure maybe it's one of those we cut loose from Whitney's camp four nights ago. What would you figure?"

"I dunno," Dawson said. "It's true—we don't know how many —if any—of those horses Whitney regathered, but I would've expected any that he didn't catch to go on downriver or head west; I wouldn't've looked for one to head for high country like this."

"Who knows what a horse will do if it gets separated and is left to run alone?" Cunningham said philosophically. "They get scared, and when that happens one might do almost anything."

"Well, I reckon that's true. . . ."

"Sure it is. And anyway, what difference does it make? We've still got to come up with those pack animals of ours. If there are three horses there when we find them, fine. We'll have found the ones we want, and that's what counts. Right?"

"Yeah," Dawson said, a bit distractedly. "I guess so."

Cunningham moved toward his horse. "Good. Let's go, then."

Dawson watched the other man swing astride, then turned as if to follow suit. But for a moment he just stood there, facing his horse, thinking. Perhaps it really didn't matter where that third horse had come from; one possibility was as good as another, he supposed. He had no way of knowing that the animal had, in fact, not been one of those left lost on the river four nights before; that it was Anson Leggitt's stray horse; that it had come within a fraction of being hauled down by the bear just that morning before breaking its reins to run away; and that as proof of this it carried three deep and painful claw marks on its rump where the bear had swiped at it as it pulled loose to run. Dawson didn't know this and thus would not be intrigued by the fact. But he wasn't comfortable with the situation as it stood, either. His mind remained on their backtrail.

Slowly he mounted, but still he looked back rather than ahead.

"What's the matter?" Cunningham demanded impatiently. "Something bothering you?"

Dawson turned to the fore. "Well, yeah, as a matter of fact, something is. . . ."

Cunningham's eyes narrowed appreciably. "What, exactly?"

"Well, the way the bear acted back there, for one thing. The way it quit the trail so suddenlike and all—like maybe it knew we were trailin' it. . . . I sure don't like that, Garst. I don't like it at all."

Cunningham only scoffed at this. "Don't worry about it. The bear doesn't know anything. We lost him, is all. Right now, we've got to find those horses—that's the first thing. Later, we'll go back to worrying about the bear."

"Yeah," Dawson mumbled to himself as he spurred his horse forward at last. "Yeah. . . ." But he still didn't like it. Dammit, he just did not!

They finally caught up with the horses about two hours later. Midafternoon had come and gone and the shadows were growing long. One horse still wore its empty packsaddle properly located atop and behind its withers; the second stood nearby, grazing, its saddle having slipped and now hanging upside down beneath its belly. The horse no longer seemed particularly excited by the encumbrance, but undoubtedly this was only because it had long since given up trying to kick the thing loose. The third horse, a blaze-faced chestnut, grazed a few feet beyond the second and wore a bridle with its reins broken off close to the bit shanks. It did not carry a saddle.

Although the horses initially acted as if they might run, all three proved less than difficult to catch. It was Dawson who slipped a loop over the head of the chestnut, and who first noticed the three bloody gouges marking its rump.

"Somethin' damn near got this old pony, Garst," he said as he led the horse over to where Cunningham had tied one horse to a bush and was straightening the packsaddle on the second. "Look at these marks."

The rancher came over to inspect. "What do you think did it?"

Dawson only looked at him. The way the wounds were spaced, the way they looked, they almost had to be claw marks. And judging from the depth of the cuts, they could not have been made by any average claw. Dawson hardly needed to say what he thought might have done it.

Cunningham walked slowly around the horse. "Here's its brand. It's not Whitney's horse, but one of those the Englishmen bought in town for the hunt. I think this is Amos Hartwood's brand—the one he uses for his livery horses in town. . . . By God, I bet this animal does belong to the hunting party! I just bet it does!"

Dawson looked at him penetratingly. "What's it doin' with a bridle on, then?"

Cunningham stared at him. "What do you mean? What difference does that make?"

"The horses we ran off on the river were hobbled for the night. They were set out to graze. They weren't wearin' bridles."

Enlightenment came quickly to the rancher's expression. "Okay, you tell me. What *is* it doing with a bridle on?"

Dawson shrugged. Of course he didn't know either.

"Well, we don't have time to worry about it. We know that damn bear is somewhere in the vicinity. Best thing for us to do is get back to our packs, make camp, and get set to go after him again tomorrow."

Dawson glanced up at the general position of the sun. Time was running out if they were to hope to make it back to where they had stashed their gear by nightfall. He said, "Fine with me. What d'you wanta do with the extra horse?"

"Take its bridle off and turn it loose. It's no good to us. It'll probably follow along anyway, but that's all right, so long as we don't have to fool with it."

Dawson did as he was told. He released the horse, re-coiled his lariat, and a few minutes later they were on their way.

Still, they were not destined to make it back to the place where they had left their gear. Twenty-five minutes past sundown caught them having just regained the small clearing with the pretty stand of aspen and the beaver pond—yet two hours' ride from their cache. And it wasn't darkness that would stop them. It was something of much greater consequence than that.

For there, as they crossed the creek and entered the clearing just above the beaver pond, dead ahead and fully in the open, was the bear, caught dragging a fine young buck it apparently had just felled toward some hiding place or another across the way. Perhaps because the light was lessening rapidly now, and what wind there was came at their side, both the men and the bear were slow to detect each other's presence. But then one of the horses snorted, and shied. All of the horses became intensely agitated. The bear dropped its burden, turned, and woofed ill-temperedly. It started to rise to its hind feet as the two men fought to control their mounts.

And then it happened. As the bear swayed indecisively before them, Garst Cunningham swung to the ground with rifle in hand.

CHAPTER 6

THE BEAR

1

Except for the finding of Anson early on, the day had not gone well at all for June. She had been so conscious of the possibility of getting lost, so determined not to let that happen to her, that perhaps she had jinxed herself with it. Perhaps. Or maybe she was simply the victim of bad luck. Maybe it was both. Who could say?

In any event, she had become lost. Terribly so. Looking back on it, she later knew pretty much what had happened. But, as is often the case with such things, realization had come much too late with too much of the day gone to overcome the loss of time.

Actually what had happened had not been all that predictable. June had selected the downcanyon trail, hoping to find high ground rather quickly. It wasn't a bad choice, for many such trails will indeed top out before the lower reaches of the canyon are achieved. But this canyon had proven to be much longer and deeper than she had thought it would. The trail had angled toward the bottom, and once there had then stayed with that position for well over a mile. By the time they had found a way out of the canyon, over an hour had been consumed. Worse, high ground at the rim of the canyon had not really been high ground at all. Towering spruce and fir hid all but snatches of blue sky, generally seen straight above. Thus, not only were there no landmarks to be seen, directions were almost impossible to determine.

June didn't think she was disoriented at this point, but she must have been, for by the time they reached an open area where she could really see, the sun was straight up and directions were once again not that easy to discern. And still she could not locate a landmark. Because of this, she wound up steering them toward what she thought was higher ground yet, a place—any place— affording a real view.

At first more annoyed than anything else, June had soon become anxious. She knew they were not following any kind of direct course to anywhere, much less the river. But she also knew she must first get her bearings; she must locate at least one or two useful landmarks; she could not simply head west or north hoping to hit the river as it swung around. It could take forever that way, and it was even possible that they might find the river and then not know whether they were upstream or downstream from the camp. Her determination to find that right piece of high ground became so singular she could hardly think of anything else.

And so it was, at almost two hours past noon, that they finally came to a place where a good view presented itself. At first there was relief akin to exhilaration. Rising splendidly in the distance, looming there, was Squaretop Mountain. Between them and it, dipping well below both points, lay the basin through which the Blanco River flowed. From there, swinging around to their left, snaked the long, low line of the river itself. It was surprising how familiar the view was to each of them. So very, very familiar . . .

And then they realized why—at least, June and Jessica did. Only yesterday they had stood and looked at it from almost precisely this same spot. They had approached it from a slightly different angle this time, and so at first had not recognized it. But now they did, for in addition to the view, less than twenty-five yards to their right, stood a certain lightning-warped tree, and beneath it, the trail where sundown had just yesterday forced them to cease their tracking for the day. And below, at the bottom of a little canyon the trail had crossed, was the spot where the two girls had camped for the night. Dismayed, they realized that they had come almost full circle, to a point that had taken them all day yesterday to reach from the river.

And they knew then, bearings or no bearings, that there was no way they could make it back to camp—or even go halfway there—before dark.

Unhappily, they decided to at least make the start and go as far as they could following yesterday's backtrail, but they could only do so knowing that there was no hope now of avoiding another night out on the trail.

A while before sundown, they arrived at a spot where June thought they might make camp for the night. The site was good— a small clearing with a creek trickling down its center—and both the horses and their riders were bone-tired and in serious need of a rest.

"There's no use pushing ourselves any harder than we already have," she told Jessica and Anson. "Besides, I don't want to get us lost again by pushing on till dark. I've already fouled up enough on that score."

Jessica slid stiffly from behind June's saddle to the ground. "Quit blaming yourself, June. It's not your fault, and certainly it could be worse. We've found Anson—which I could never have done by myself—and we're alive. Nothing really bad has happened to us, has it?"

"Nothing, except we may yet starve to death," June observed dismally as she too dismounted, followed closely by Anson, who had ridden up right behind them with Fleck at his horse's heels. "Even with what Anson brought, we haven't much to eat, nothing to cook in, and we may or may not be able to start a fire with the few matches I have left. At all costs, this absolutely must be our last night out like this." She looked around then. "Here, Anson, help me unsaddle the horses. Jessica, see if you can find some firewood. We might as well make do the best we can."

A short while later they had completed the basic tasks of setting up a camp: The horses staked out to graze, a fire pit scratched out in the soft dirt and wood gathered, their one bedroll and their saddle blankets placed where they would make their beds for the night. June made sure their rifles were located in handy positions and was just then rummaging through her saddlebags to see what food they had left. Anson sat nearby scratching the dog's ears. Jessica lounged a few feet beyond him.

"Do you think Gil and the others will be looking for us by

now?" Jessica asked presently. "Do you think there's any chance they might find us before we get back on our own?"

June shrugged. They had quite naturally wondered about this before during the day. "If they've come back to camp yet and learned we're gone, they might. Remember, they went out after the bear with no idea when they'd return. Even if they are looking for us, the way we've wandered around could challenge a pack of hounds to find us. Which bothers me some. What if we do make it back tomorrow and they're up here hunting us? They'll be worried sick and will probably hesitate to give up the search till they've found something. Of course, that's something I should have thought of this morning when I chose the other trail. . . ."

But Anson, for one, wasn't interested in this. Something in her earlier words had caught his attention.

"Apparently the bear has been closer to us than them all along," he said suddenly. "At least I assume the beast that ran off my horse was *the* bear. Was it, June?"

"I have no idea. Actually, I guess I didn't study the tracks as well as I should have. I just know they were very big, and that they could have been those of a grizzly, very possibly Old Tuffy's. But you've got to quit worrying about that, Anson. Whatever it was, it's probably miles away from here by now. Chances are we'll never see it again, believe me."

"Yeah, well, I certainly hope so," Anson grumbled, although sounding somewhat less than convinced.

"Don't worry," June repeated. "Besides, we've got the dog to warn us if anything comes around again. Like as not, anything that does will turn right around and go the other way the minute Fleck sets up barking. And like I told you, that old bear is probably long gone from here by now. Why, I suspect there is almost no chance we'll run into him two nights in a row. Almost no chance at all."

June had no idea whether this pronouncement was true or not; she hardly even thought about that aspect of it. Her sole intent was to reassure Anson. She wasn't trying to be prophetic.

Which was just as well, for it was less than half an hour past sunset when they heard a shot ring loudly out from somewhere beyond the trees that bordered the lower end of the clearing. A second shot followed, and June was almost certain that neither could have been fired from more than a quarter of a mile away.

2

Gil, Buck, and Sir Robert had at first made good time in their effort to follow June and Jessica's trail. They had left camp as soon as there was adequate light and had cleared the first eastward bench leading uphill from the river by sunup. But the trail soon became, if anything, even more confusing for them than it must have been for June and Jessica the day before. Plainly they were following three sets of tracks—two made always atop another, the two girls undoubtedly following Anson. But they had gone hither and yon, wandering erratically over trails that for a while led them southward, then eastward, then back south, and finally to the east once again.

On more than one occasion the first set of tracks went subtly one way, the second two another. Each time, the three men witnessed how the second pair had quickly backtracked to where they had become separated from the first set of tracks. Not once did they completely lose the trail.

Still, the difficulties for the three men were many. The land rose in a series of broad, slightly sloping benches going east and south from the river. The trail took Gil and his companions higher and higher. Deer and elk used the paths that Anson and the two girls had followed, sometimes covering over the tracks with their own. It was never easy staying with the right trail. The three men no longer made good time.

The day passed swiftly. As best the trackers could tell, they had traveled perhaps fifteen miles to go no more than four or five, in a straight line, from the river. And still they had found neither the two girls nor Anson. Nonetheless, although they did not know it, they had at least made better time than June and Jessica had made the day before. At about four o'clock they found where someone had made a night camp alongside a tiny stream at the base of a brushy hill with a lightning-warped pine at its top. They came to the top of the hill, viewed Squaretop, the river and the basin, just as the girls had on more than one occasion now. There was a good deal of confusion in the tracks here, for two sets came and went, then came again before going off the hill on its other side, seemingly once more following the first set. And neither Gil nor Buck saw, twenty-five yards away, where two sets had yet another time—barely two hours earlier—approached the hill from another direction, and had left it on what was a slight and unintentional, but nonetheless adequate, departure from the original trail. The men just did not see this, either.

Thus, unaware that they were taking the long way around, Gil and his companions followed yesterday's tracks on past the hill to where Anson had camped, found there the remnants of the bear's tracks and the boot tracks of three people, two of which plainly were the girls'. They also found what was left of Anson's bridle reins tied to a bush and one set of horse tracks leaving at a run in one direction, while two others followed the trail on down the canyon, going in another. Unable to tell for sure where the bear had gone, they worriedly debated what to do, before finally deciding to take the downcanyon trail.

They trailed along steadily but became increasingly aware as they went that they would in a couple of hours run out of daylight altogether. Finally they topped out in the dense forest bordering the canyon rim, only to find once again a trail that wandered erratically here and there without evident destination.

Now they made poorer time than ever. Someone up ahead had become badly lost, and anyone could see why. Even Gil felt lost, for he could not locate a helpful landmark anywhere. Worse yet, they lost the trail and had to backtrack, trying desperately to pick it up again. They wandered northward, abandoning their own backtrail, went much farther than they had intended. Sundown caught them having gone unknowingly away from the brushy hill where June and the others had finally regained their bearings before heading west again. And in having this happen, they made what was to become a truly fortunate error. For in wandering from the trail at what should have been the worst of times, when dark might catch them with no way to pick it up again until the next day, they accidently cut across to a point closer than they had been all day to finding the two girls and Anson.

The only trouble was, there in the densest forest they had seen yet, they had no way of knowing this. Like two ships passing in the night, the two parties might have camped but half a mile apart and never have known it—had they not, a short while later, heard the two shots go ringing through the hills, shattering the stillness of the fading day.

3

From the moment Cunningham and Riddle rode up on the bear, things happened too fast to Dawson for him to ever have a significant impact on their outcome. First, he never could get his frightened mount under control. The horse simply came apart beneath him. Dawson found himself doing all he could just to hold on as the animal bucked wildly out across the clearing and away from the bear.

Fear controlled them both, but unfortunately for Dawson, while the horse was crazed with it, Dawson was simply made weak by it. He never had a chance. On the fifth or sixth jump, he suddenly went flying. He landed hard, so hard his breath went *whoosh* and pain wracked him in his back and his ribs. Then, as he lay there gasping desperately for air, seeing funny flashing lights he knew were not stars, he heard Cunningham's first shot. Dully, he rolled over on his stomach, trying desperately through pain-bleared eyes to see what was happening.

Still gasping, he at first made out two dim forms, one much larger and moving, the second standing still. A second shot sounded, and Dawson saw the flame as it left the rifle barrel. His eyes cleared as his brain struggled to take in what he saw.

And then it struck him. Cunningham had somehow become dismounted and was facing the bear on foot. None of the horses were anywhere to be seen. Cunningham had fired at the bear, twice now, but he had not downed it. The two were less than twenty-five yards apart and the bear was charging.

Dawson struggled to get up, made it to his knees. Cunningham seemed to be struggling with his rifle . . . the bear closing the distance between them with startling rapidity. Horrified, Dawson could only watch as the huge animal was suddenly upon the man with the rifle, who only at the last minute flung the weapon at the bear's head and tried to turn and run. But too late . . . he was much too late. He went down beneath the bear's weight and disappeared. Dawson heard him scream hoarsely, heard the bear roar and growl, saw it cuff viciously at its tormentor of only moments before.

In desperation, Dawson looked around for his rifle. It was still in his saddle scabbard, gone with his horse. He had no sidearm. He was helpless to do anything. He had a knife, but what could he possibly hope to do with that? Helpless . . . he was utterly helpless.

Cunningham's screams were both horror- and pain-filled. Already sick to his stomach from the impact of the fall, Dawson suddenly began to tremble, feeling as if he might throw up, his legs so weak he could not even come to a standing position. He simply knelt there, frozen, watching and listening to the awful scene before him.

And then Cunningham ceased screaming. The bear ceased its pummeling and biting and clawing; it ceased to growl. It turned to look around. Dawson sank slowly down, frightened more than ever now. Barely fifty yards separated him from the animal . . . *it might attack him next!*

Dawson Riddle wanted to rise and run—oh, how desperately he wanted to do that! But he couldn't move. His muscles felt about as sturdy as raw egg white; his breathing came, if anything, with greater labor than before. For a long, slow moment the bear seemed to look straight at him. He wished he could disappear, but he felt as large and conspicuous as a horse as he knelt there in the dying light of the day. Miraculously, the bear, with its poor eyesight, did not seem to notice him. And if it smelled him, it may have confused his scent with that of poor Cunningham. It woofed almost pathetically, tried to lick its left shoulder, seemed actually to whine. Then Dawson remembered the two shots Cunningham had fired. The bear must have been hit. But, if so, it apparently had not been badly hurt by it. Enough to anger it, to put it in a pain-crazed mood, to make that mood even worse as time went on, but not enough to greatly hinder it.

Dear God, Dawson thought, *don't let it know I'm here. Dear God. . . .*

The bear turned, shuffled back over to where it had dropped the deer carcass, sniffed at it disinterestedly. Finally it sank down on its haunches and just sat there. Again Dawson thought he heard the animal whine, like a stunned child that was in pain and could not understand why. It licked its shoulder, rose, walked around the deer carcass, was plainly ill at ease. For several minutes more Dawson watched without moving. The bear seemed undecided what to do, unwilling to leave its kill but somehow lacking the interest in it to go ahead and feed on it or carry it off. What was left of the day's light faded further, and Dawson began to wonder what he was going to do when full dark arrived and he had only moonlight by which to find his way around. Still he was afraid to make a move.

Suddenly the bear swung its head around and looked off into the forest to Dawson's right. As if alarmed, it woofed a couple of times, then quite abruptly whirled and lumbered off toward the upper end of the clearing. Dawson, stunned, watched as the bear disappeared in the trees and the poor light, then turned to look for himself at what must have frightened the bear.

At first he saw nothing. Then he heard a crashing in the brush, hoofbeats, and finally saw three riders come bursting into the open. Afraid they might not see him, he jumped instantly to his feet and began waving his arms and yelling:

"Hey! Hey, fellers, over here! It's me—Dawson Riddle! I just watched the damned bear kill Cunningham!"

4

It took several minutes to get Riddle settled down, and when they did he then led them over to where Cunningham's body lay hidden in the tall grass and weeds. Gil dismounted, followed closely by Sir Robert and Buck, to make sure the rancher was not somehow yet alive. He was not, and even in the near darkness the sight was almost too gruesome to behold.

Gil shook his head and turned away. "That's awful."

Buck looked over at a still shaken Dawson Riddle. "Did you just stand and watch this happen? Didn't you try to do something?"

"I told you I didn't have no gun," Dawson said sullenly. "My horse ran off with my rifle. What'd you want me to do, go over and tackle the son of a bitch by hand? I'd've only got killed myself. By God, I would!"

"He's right, Buck," Gil said. "There was nothing he could do. Where's your horse now, Dawson? Where's Cunningham's horse?"

"Hell, I dunno," the other man grumbled. "We had two pack-horses followin' us, and another one that got away from your party. I dunno where any of 'em went. Just to hell and gone outa here, I reckon. Anything to get away from the bear."

"Good heavens!" Sir Robert exclaimed from nearby. "Do you suppose this same thing happened to poor Anson?" He was looking, despite himself, back down at the body of Cunningham and framing the obvious mental picture as he did.

Gil turned on Dawson. "Did you know that Anson Leggitt was wandering around up here alone? That June and Jessica St. John set out alone to find him? Have you seen any of them?"

"Now, how in hell could I know anything like that? And hell no, I ain't seen 'em. Why—"

He didn't finish, for suddenly Buck Blaine held up a silencing hand. "Ssssh! Listen. Did you hear that?"

"What?" Gil asked. "I didn't hear anything."

"A scream . . . I'd swear it was a woman's scream."

Gil gave him a skeptical look. "A mountain lion maybe—"

But Buck shook his head vigorously. "No . . . I'm sure it wasn't that." Once again he listened. "And that, too. Did you hear it? A dog barking. Dammit, I know it was!"

This time Gil did hear. Faintly, very faintly, it came to him through the still forest air—from the east, beyond the head of the clearing, almost beyond earshot—a dog barking!

"Fleck!" Gil said suddenly. "That could be Fleck!"

Buck turned quickly to his horse. "C'mon!" he yelled.

Gil and Sir Robert did not hesitate. Instantly they were at their mounts and swinging astride.

Only Dawson Riddle failed to make a move to follow along. He couldn't. He had no mount. "Hey! What about me? You're not gonna leave me here, are you?"

Buck reined around impatiently, then proffered an arm down. "Here—climb on behind me. But dammit, hurry up, or I sure as hell will leave you!"

One thing that could be said for Dawson Riddle: In such situations, he wasted no time. With but precious few seconds lost, he was aboard behind Buck, and they were soon racing through the darkened forest in the direction of the dog's barking.

The moon, full now in its cycle, rose bright and gleaming in the east as the last traces of daylight faded from the sky behind them. But the going remained difficult. They were forced to pick their way among pitch-black shadows mixed with open patches of moonlight, in and around underbrush, over fallen logs, back and forth across the creek that fed the beaver pond behind them, and their pace was difficult to maintain.

But they did not waver from their course; they did not slow down. Up ahead, the dog continued to bark, the sounds coming to them louder now, but with less excitement than before. A little farther and they picked up the glow of a campfire flickering beyond the trees. Moments after this they came to a small clearing, at the head of which the campfire now danced brightly in full view. A little closer and they saw that beside the fire stood June, rifle in hand and white of face. Nearby, Jessica and Anson struggled to hold two horses that were obviously nervous to the point of fright. Barely within the fire's circle of light dashed the dog, still barking—now as much as anything at the approaching riders, but at the same time plainly hesitating to completely relinquish its position along the camp's far perimeter.

June set her rifle down and was in Gil's arms the moment he rode up and leaped to the ground. "Gil! Oh, Gil . . . I almost can't believe it! Was that you shooting a while ago? Was it the bear you shot at?" She released herself and backed away as the others also pulled up and began to dismount. "Buck? Is that you, Buck? And Sir Robert . . . and Dawson Riddle? Where did *you* come from? Oh, I can't believe any of this!"

Gil gave her a sober look. "It wasn't us doing the shooting, June. It was Garst Cunningham. The bear killed him. Dawson was there, but he had no gun and was forced to stand by and watch. We got there too late to do any good."

The two girls and the young man who was their companion exchanged horrified expressions. "Garst . . . dead?" June's voice was almost a whisper. "Oh, Gil, you can't mean that!"

"I'm afraid I do, June. He fired twice, but according to Dawson, his rifle must have jammed as the bear charged. I'm sorry; it is terrible, but there's nothing we can do about it now. You asked if I had shot at the bear. . . ." He looked past her, into the night. "Is that what's out there? Did you *see* the bear?"

The girl nodded affirmatively. "It was awful. We heard the shooting but didn't know what to do. We were still waiting to see if there would be any more shots when suddenly the bear charged out of the night, coming almost into camp with us. I think only Fleck's barking caused it to stop. I had my rifle ready, but the bear ran off so fast I didn't get a shot. Maybe I was lucky, I don't know. Maybe if I'd wounded it, it really would have charged."

"From the way Dawson tells it," Buck interposed, "I'd guess that it already was wounded. You're lucky it didn't come on in, no matter what you did."

"I'd about swear to that part," Riddle put in. "Cunningham's shots were point-blank, and I know he didn't miss, 'cause the bear kept lickin' its shoulder afterward. The old devil was hurtin', I know he was."

"The sad thing is," Gil concluded, "if Garst hadn't shot at it, he might never have been attacked."

Sir Robert gave him a puzzled look at this. "But that's what we're all up here for, isn't it, Whitney? To shoot the bear? I mean, after all, what would you have expected him to do?"

Gil shrugged. "It's not just that he shot. He put himself on foot much too close to the bear and without anyone to back him. Or maybe he didn't realize until too late that Dawson wasn't going to be able to help him out. I don't know. In any event, he must have become rattled and didn't make his first shot count the way it should have. I think he wanted too badly to make the kill and took a risk that probably cost him his life—something I believe he could have avoided if he'd stayed with his horse."

Sir Robert seemed soberly intrigued by this. "You actually believe the bear wouldn't have charged if Cunningham hadn't shot at it first?"

Again Gil shrugged. "I can't say that for certain, of course. For one thing, I wasn't there and didn't see it happen. For another, grizzlies are just too damned unpredictable. But Old Tuffy has never made an unprovoked attack on a human being that I know of—never. I think even Dawson will agree with that."

It was Dawson's turn to shrug, an indication at least that he couldn't think of any exception to it, his own experiences included.

Sir Robert shook his head sadly. "Well, I suppose this hunt of mine has come to be a pretty sorry mess, hasn't it? We've a man killed, horses and such lost, our bloody selves placed in miserable circumstances. . . . By Jove, I just never thought of it turning out like this. I just never did."

Gil started to say something, but was prevented from doing so by Jessica, who suddenly stepped forward. "Gil, forgive me, but I've got to ask. That man, Cunningham. . . . Are—are you just going to leave his body out there? I mean, shouldn't something be done? Shouldn't he be buried or something?"

Gil stared at her, then around at the others. "I guess I just hadn't thought that far yet, Jessica. But you're right, of course. We'll have to go back and bury him. The body would be in horrible shape long before we could carry it all the way to Garst's ranch or to town. And Garst had no family in these parts that I know of. In the morning, I suppose, we could—"

"Oh, Gil! *In the morning?*" June suddenly looked horrified. "You mean leave him out there all night? Possibly for some animal to come along and—and . . ." The thought was so revolting to her she couldn't even finish the sentence.

Gil sighed, knowing full well how she felt. The body hadn't been in good shape after the bear had finished with it, but to think what might happen to it if some forest scavenger happened along was almost too much. He and Garst had had their differences, but Gil was not happy to see the other man dead, and now that he thought about it, he did not like the thought of leaving the body out there overnight any more than June seemed to.

Trouble was, if someone went back now, who should go and who should stay?

"I don't want to leave this camp unprotected again," he told them. "Not tonight with that bear maybe still prowling around out there." He looked at Buck. "I suppose either you or I could go and bring the body here where we could watch over it until morning. Or maybe we could even bury it tonight, whatever seems best. If you want, I'll go back and—"

"Oh no, Gil!" June objected instantly. "Not just you alone. What if *you* run into the bear?"

"She's right, Gil," Buck said. "At least two oughta go."

Gil thought about it for a moment, then said, "Okay, Sir Robert and I will go. You stay here with the others, Buck. We'll take three horses—one to carry the body back on and two to ride—and we'll come straight back as soon as we've got the body in tow. Is that okay with you, Sir Robert?"

The Englishman, not one to shirk a duty, said instantly, "Absolutely. You can bloody well count on me, Whitney."

"Good. First let's get something to eat and help set this camp up a little better—straighten out the bedding situation and such— then we'll go." He glanced down at Fleck, now having finally relaxed his vigil near the camp's perimeter to come and plop down at Gil's feet. "Buck, you keep the dog here. He'll warn you if the bear comes back. I don't think it'll take over an hour for Sir Robert and me to get back here with the body, and if somebody wants to help out while we're gone, there's a camp shovel on my saddle that can be used to get started on the grave."

"I'll help with that," a heretofore quiet Anson Leggitt volunteered. "I'd like to do something, at least."

"Thanks, Anson," Gil told him sincerely. Then he looked around. "Okay, let's stop wasting time, then. Someone get some more wood and build up that fire. Buck, June, Jessica, what have we got to eat? I don't want to be at this all night, so let's get a move on. Okay?"

To this only a deeply preoccupied Dawson Riddle failed to respond. He stood off to one side and was hardly listening. Something quite a lot more intriguing than either fixing up the camp or eating supper had just occurred to him. Somehow though, in the commotion that followed, the fact of his preoccupation went unnoticed by Gil and the others. It was too bad that it did.

Just over an hour later, Gil and Sir Robert left the camp. They led Jessica's horse, saddled, and had brought along an extra lariat rope and a tarp from Gil's bedroll, with which they would tie on and cover the body when they got there.

"Are you sure we can find the way back?" Sir Robert asked as they left the clearing and entered the trees.

"No problem," Gil said. "All we have to do is follow the creek. It'll be easier than before, believe me."

And it was. The moon was well up in the sky now and thus provided even more light and not quite such long shadows as before. And their pace was more sensible, their way more selective. It would take a few minutes longer to get there, but their arrival would be much more sure this way.

Nevertheless, something now had become very difficult to describe about the forest. Something eerie that both of them must have felt but only Sir Robert voiced.

"I'm not the sort to be afraid of the dark, Whitney. Surely you know that by now. But, by Jove, this is a bloody strange night we're having here. It's got me a bit on the old edge, I'll tell you."

"It's not every night you go out to bring in a corpse," Gil pointed out. "That's enough to make anyone nervous."

"You mean it does you, too?"

Gil smiled. "Yeah. Me, too."

They rode along in silence for a while, Gil leading the extra horse, Sir Robert coming along slightly behind.

"You know, Whitney," the Englishman called ahead presently, "this business has really put me to thinking. I imagine we'll be going back to the river camp tomorrow, and after that we're going to have to make what I suspect will be a rather difficult decision as to what to do next. Don't you think?"

Gil cocked his head at this, but did not look back. "You mean whether to continue the hunt or not?"

"Yes. That precisely."

Gil shrugged. "That'll be up to you, Sir Robert. You're paying me to guide you, and if you want to go on with it, I won't back out on you. Of course, if you decide to quit, we'd be giving up the bounty money—at least I would—but that wouldn't matter. I never counted on that in the first place. I'll gladly go along with whatever you decide."

"I appreciate that, Whitney," the Englishman said in deep sincerity. "I really do."

Again they rode in silence, this time until they had almost arrived at the head of the clearing. They were yet within the cover of the trees when suddenly Gil reined to a halt, his eyes locked on something he saw in the middle of the clearing—bathed now in moonlight so bright it was almost as if the sun had come back up.

"What is it, Whitney?" Sir Robert asked in a low voice as he pulled up beside Gil. "Why are we stopping?"

"Sssssh! Look out there—in the middle of the clearing, to the left of the pond. Do you see it?"

The Englishman squinted hard, then said, "Oh, my God! The bear, Whitney? My God, is that the bear?"

Gil nodded affirmatively. The animal was perhaps seventy yards away, and did not seem to have seen them. But there was no question what it was. Its coat was frosty, there in the moonlight, and the animal was big, very big. The bear, of course.

"My God," the Englishman repeated, almost dumb struck. "What's it doing here? Why hasn't it seen us?"

"I don't know. I suspect he's come back for that deer he killed. He's busy with that and just hasn't caught our scent or heard us yet. And look—we better get these horses away from here before the bear does see us, or before one of them gets *his* scent and gives us away. Come on—follow me and be quiet."

Cautiously they reined around and retraced their steps. When they reached a point that was fully out of sight of the clearing, Gil quickly dismounted and began tying his horse to a bush. Sir Robert instinctively followed suit. "What are we going to do, Whitney? Are we going back there? On foot?"

Gil, having finished tying the second horse a few yards away from the first, was now removing his rifle from its saddle scabbard. As quietly as possible, he levered a shell into the firing chamber. He said to the Englishman, "You still want your chance at the bear, don't you?"

"Well . . . yes. I suppose I do. . . ."

"Okay, then. It'll have to be right now, while we still have him more or less unaware. It's not the kind of chance that'll wait long, or possibly will ever come again. So be quick. Grab your rifle and let's go."

For the briefest of moments it seemed as if the Englishman was not going to move. But then he seemed to square his shoulders, as if working to regather his resolve, and turned to pull his rifle from its scabbard. Seconds later, they were quietly making their way on foot back toward the clearing.

As they came within full view of the opening once more, Gil stopped, sank to one knee, and motioned for Sir Robert to do the same.

"He's still there," he whispered, pointing. "But he's moved; he's closer now. He must be dragging the deer this way."

Very slowly, trying to make as little sound as possible, the Englishman worked the bolt of his rifle. Both men sank down even farther as the bear suddenly picked up the deer carcass and resumed its movement. Sure enough, the beast was coming their way. Nervously, Sir Robert started to raise his rifle.

"Hold it," Gil cautioned with what was the barest of whispers. "We've got to get set. That first shot has to be a telling one or we'll never bring him down. Here, that log over there—use it for a gun rest. I'll set up beside you, in case he charges and you need the backing."

Sir Robert inched his way forward. He didn't have far to go, and presently he lay belly flat with his rifle rested atop the log. He looked back as Gil followed his lead and was soon in a similar position, two yards to his left. Ready now, both men renewed their concentration on the clearing before them.

But now the bear had stopped again. Somewhere between forty and fifty yards away, it had dropped its burden and was simply standing on all fours with its nose to the air, its massive head turning first one way then the other.

"What's he doing?" Sir Robert whispered. "Why does he keep stopping? Is he tired?"

Gil wagged his head thoughtfully. "I doubt that. But he may be hurting. Remember, Dawson said he thought one of Cunningham's bullets caught him in the left shoulder. He does seem to limp a little, now that I think about it."

But as much as Gil would like to think it, he knew this wasn't the most likely reason the animal kept hesitating, why it kept lifting its nose to the air the way it did. He turned his eyes toward the beaver pond, the head of which was now about even with the bear's position. Its moonlit surface was perfectly still, glassy; the forest was almost completely without a breeze. Could the bear have caught their scent anyway? Could it have heard something?

"Should I shoot now?" Sir Robert wanted to know. "Or should I let him come closer?"

"Let him come closer. In daylight, we'd take him where he is. But just now I'd like to make sure we get a better shot. Just be patient. He's coming again. Watch."

Once more the bear settled its huge jaws about the neck of the dead deer, began dragging it toward them. And no question about it: The animal *was* limping, even laboring some now under its burden. Perhaps it was even more seriously injured than Gil had thought. Chances were the wounded shoulder had had time to stiffen by now, and it was altogether possible that the bear had lost enough blood to weaken it. Conceivably, this condition might reduce the animal's ferociousness, might make it more vulnerable to attack . . . conceivably. *But that's still a grizzly out there,* Gil reminded himself. Nothing could be taken for granted. Absolutely nothing.

Slowly, Gil sighted down his rifle barrel, testing his sights against the moonlight. Still, he would rather the bear come closer. He had every intention of giving Sir Robert the first shot, and he had confidence in the man's ability to shoot. But that shot must be a good one, as must any backup shots Gil himself might need to take. The bear must not be so close they could not fell it in mid-charge, if necessary; but it must not be so far away that the sights could not be fixed clearly on the target. Closer, perhaps ten yards . . . that would be enough.

But the bear had stopped again, dropping the deer carcass and raising its nose to once more sniff the air. Only this time it seemed more attentive, almost alarmed. Ears sharply erect, it looked clearly in their direction. Gil thought he could hear a throaty growl, imagined those tiny piglike eyes straining against the night.

"He's seen us, Whitney." Sir Robert's voice was a hoarse whisper. "He knows we're here!"

"Sight in on him," Gil said. "But don't fire until I tell you. Let's make sure what he's going to do."

The bear looked to its left, then back dead ahead. It seemed to whimper. It looked down at the deer carcass, then again to its left. It seemed confused. And so was Gil. He just could not figure out the bear's actions.

Sir Robert tightened his grip on his rifle, sighted down its length for what seemed a long several seconds, then raised his head and lessened his grip. He looked at Gil. "I can't do it, Whitney. I can't shoot."

"W-what? You can't do what?"

There was agony in the Englishman's voice. "I can't go through with it. After all this, I cannot shoot that bear. I just cannot."

Gil stared at him. "My God, you must be kidding! You came all the way here, went through all we've gone through—*and now you can't shoot the bear?*"

Sir Robert shook his head. "This has never happened to me before, Whitney. Believe me, it hasn't. But that is a magnificent animal out there. And it's done very little wrong, except to kill a few cows and defend itself when put upon in every way conceivable by man. I have never observed its like anywhere in the world—not in Africa, nor India, nor anywhere in Europe or America. I cannot shoot that bear!"

Astonished, Gil returned his gaze to the clearing. The bear still stood there, seemingly frozen over its kill, as yet unsure of what to do. The tiniest breeze suddenly caused aspen leaves to flutter in the moonlight; the bear remained unmoving. Gil thought again about what Sir Robert had just said. Somehow, strangely, he could not disagree. Finally, he, too, relaxed his grip on his rifle.

But then something happened. The bear suddenly became even more alert than before, swinging its attention quickly to its left, toward the edge of the clearing. It gave a sort of grunt, followed by a throaty growl. Something had moved within the aspens; a form appeared suddenly in the full moonlight not two dozen

yards from where Garst Cunningham's body had been left . . . a
human form!

"What the hell . . . ?" Gil breathed in astonishment. "Who is
that?"

Sir Robert, too, had seen. But for once the Englishman seemed
speechless. Then the bear growled again as something flashed
dimly in the moonlight; Gil and Sir Robert, lying motionless,
could only watch as flame suddenly spurted and the tremendous
shock of a rifle shot reverberated across the clearing.

The bear, roaring with what must have been instant pain and
anger, whirled toward its attacker and was in full charge by the
time the second shot rang out. Gil, realizing there was less than
fifty yards between the two, finally became mobilized. Scrambling
quickly to his feet, he yelled at Sir Robert, "Hurry! We've got to
help him bring it down. Quick—before it gets to him!"

Three rifles boomed in rapid succession, then boomed again.
The bear seemed to swerve slightly but did not slow down. Gil
grabbed Sir Robert's arm as the animal closed the gap between it
and its first tormentor. The angle was suddenly such that the bear
was almost in line with the man at the aspens' edge. Gil said,
"Come on. Follow me."

They took off running. The figure near the trees fired again,
began to retreat backward, fired once more. The bear roared, fal-
tering almost imperceptibly, but otherwise did not slow down. Another shot rang out. Gil veered to the right, trying to stay out of
the line of fire; Sir Robert's footsteps sounded immediately behind him.

The man at the edge of the trees seemed to be struggling with
his rifle now, perhaps having emptied it. Gil kept on running—but
so did the bear, despite the fact that it must now know it was
being attacked from more than one side. The man gave up fooling
with his rifle and belatedly turned to run. But too late. Before he
had taken two steps, the bear was upon him and down he went.
Gil and Sir Robert, yet twenty yards away and not knowing what
else was left for them to do, instinctively pulled up and raised
their rifles—only to find that suddenly there was no target. The
man was down, all right, but the bear had disappeared!

Gil and Sir Robert gawked as they realized that the animal had not stopped to pummel its victim. Instead, amazingly, it had kept right on running. They could still hear it crashing through the brush and trees beyond the clearing's edge—they could hear it but they could no longer see it, and they knew it was gone.

Moments later the crashing in the brush had faded, and there was only silence from within the trees as Gil and Sir Robert came running up to find a white-faced Dawson Riddle just getting to his feet. Apparently little hurt, the man mumbled, "Hell, I thought the bastard was gonna kill me, but all he did was knock me down and just keep on runnin'!"

Sir Robert looked at him in pure astonishment. "My God, man! Where did you come from? And whose gun is that there? I thought you'd lost yours."

"It's Miss June's," Riddle admitted frankly as he reached a shaky hand down to retrieve the fallen weapon. "I reckon I took it. I sorta thought that old bear would come back here for its kill, and I wanted my crack at it in case you guys missed yours." He paused, breathing deeply and shakily. "I waited till no one was watchin', then took the rifle and slipped off. Come all the way here on foot, I did; ran all the way. And I thought I had the bastard. I emptied the gun on him and he still wouldn't go down. He almost got *me!*"

Gil just stared at him. "Didn't you know we were over there? Didn't you know you opened up on him while we were still sighting in?" He saw no reason to tell Dawson that they had all but decided not to shoot. That part didn't change the fact that the man had intruded upon what might have been theirs to do first.

"Hell, no," Riddle answered quickly, and probably honestly. "How could I know where you was at? Not until you started shootin', anyways. I saw the bear and I figured I saw my chance. He was leavin' the clearin' and wasn't gonna get any closer to me, so I took my shot. I just can't believe the son of a gun didn't go down, I just can't."

"Surely the beast must have been hit," Sir Robert said then. "All of those shots couldn't have missed, could they?"

Gil shook his head. "No. You can tell a shot that hits home; there's a duller sound, almost a thud. I'd swear that bear took no less than four or five slugs. Enough to kill any animal at that range, even a grizzly."

"You think he might still die, then? That even though he didn't go down here, he still might, somewhere out there?"

"I think so," Gil said. "Many's the time a wounded animal has done that: Lived to run away only to die later. The only thing that surprises me is that he kept going after he reached Dawson. Any other bear, grizzly or black, would have been crazed to the point it would have stayed to maul its attacker no matter what the danger from some other quarter. I never thought I'd see one with the sense to keep running the way this one did."

"But how will we know if he's alive or dead?" Sir Robert asked. "We can't go out there looking for him *now*, can we?"

"No, not now." Gil's brow furrowed as he thought about it. "Not in the dark. Maybe in the morning . . . we might find out then."

"Do you think it actually was the silver bear?"

Gil shrugged. "I don't know. For sure, he was big enough. . . ."

"I *know* it was him," Dawson Riddle put in. "I've seen him before enough times to know it couldn't've been no other. I'd swear to that."

Gil looked out across the moonlit clearing. "Well, in any case, we'll find out tomorrow when we can see his tracks. Right now, we'd better get on with what we came here to do, then get on back to camp. I'm sure the others heard the shooting and will be worried about it. Sir Robert, you and Dawson go get the horses; I'll see if I can find Garst's body."

Still, Sir Robert hesitated. "But what if the bear doesn't die, Whitney? What if he's still alive out there? Do you think he'll come back, that he might still represent some danger to us?"

Gil's pause was nothing more than a thoughtful mental shrug. "I think the bear will die, Sir Robert. If not right away, then soon. Tomorrow, we'll try to track him down and find out. If he's still alive, we'll finish him; if not . . . well, at least we'll know. We'll know once and for all the fate of the silver bear."

5

An hour later they reappeared at camp, Dawson Riddle once again riding double, this time behind Gil. They found there a worried audience who had indeed heard the shots and had been waiting anxiously—it had been all he could do for Buck to restrain himself from going to find out for himself—for an answer as to what had happened. The story was told after they buried Garst Cunningham's body about fifty yards away from the camp; finding no one sleepy among them, they stayed up late talking about it around the campfire. The questions were endless. Was it really Old Tuffy that had been encountered? Was he dead by now or not? Would they ever know for sure?

The next day they returned to the clearing to try to find out. They caught all three of Cunningham's horses, found grazing nearby. This was fortunate, for they needed the horses, but it did not serve to help them much with their primary objective—that of learning what had happened to the bear.

They found plenty of tracks; they found telltale forepaw prints with all of the proper toes missing; they even found blood, dried and caking now, but plenty of blood nevertheless. The bear *had* been Old Tuffy; and he *had* been hit—perhaps badly, judging from the amount of blood found.

But where was he? They tried tracking him. At first this wasn't difficult. The tracks were clear, the blood having poured profusely. The bear had left the clearing at a lumbering run, going almost due north. But then it had peeled left and had curled back around until it was headed south again, and the tracking became more difficult as the blood lessened.

After a while the bear had come to the creek about three hundred yards below the beaver dam. Here it had wallowed in the cool water and mud, perhaps in treatment of its wounds. Then it had continued on south, no longer leaving a consistent blood trail and moving now at a steady but slower pace. They followed along for perhaps a mile, finding all the while less and less sign that the animal had still been bleeding. What had been an occasional splotch now became only a rare drop, and finally there was no longer even that. And then they came to a bouldery, rock-strewn hillside on which there were not even any tracks. The trail simply stopped, and try as they might, they could not pick it up again. Even the dog, which had been following the bear's scent, suddenly seemed at a loss as to where their quarry had gone.

After about two hours of fruitless searching, Gil reluctantly told the others, "We've lost him. He must have jumped from boulder to boulder until he broke his scent trail enough to lose even Fleck. And he's quit bleeding. We can stay at it longer if you want, but I think it would be pure luck if we found him now."

"You mean he's got away again?" Sir Robert asked in disbelief. "He's gone, just like that?"

"I'm afraid so. And there's little telling where to. By now, he could've crawled off someplace to die . . . or, if he's still alive, maybe he's holed up for the day. Either way, he'd be hard as the devil to find."

"Do you think now that he might not die of his wounds after all?" Sir Robert's eyes were bright with what might almost have been termed hope.

At this Gil could only shrug. He was beginning to wonder, he really was. The bear had bled heavily at first; it must have been hit hard. But where was the blood now? Where was the bear? Gil simply did not know what to make of it.

"Do you want to keep on looking?" he asked the Englishman.

Sir Robert thought for several moments, then simply shook his head. "I hate to leave a wounded animal to die a slow death . . . but as you say, we'd have to be very lucky to find him now. And I don't want to hunt him anymore. The way I felt last night has not been diminished a bit by what's happened since. Not one bit. My feeling is, if he dies, well, we can't help that now. But if he lives, by Jove, I say let him live. I want no more part of trying to do in that magnificent animal. No part of it at all. For me, the hunt is over. Over and done with. Does anyone disagree?"

No one did. Even Dawson Riddle, who had by now had time to fully contemplate the fact that three times he had faced the bear head-on and three times had been lucky to come away with his own life, no longer seemed inclined to continue. Without further discussion, the party turned to go back. As Sir Robert had said, the hunt for the bear was over. It was over for all of them. They knew they were going home.

6

Very late that afternoon they arrived back at the river camp, where they told their story to a rapt and disbelieving Sir Henry, the two English ladies, and Antonio. Midafternoon, two days later, they arrived back at Gil's ranch, and four days after that drove to town with Gil, Buck, Antonio, June, and even Sir Henry doing the driving of the wagons and surreys. In town, the hunting party once again set out to hire drivers for the trip back to Durango.

Early the following morning they were assembled in front of Bud Sampson's store, getting ready to say their good-byes. Sir Robert had just come from the post office, where he had left word with friends and family to write him while he was gone. He carried with him, among other things, a letter from Stuart Gladney, the New York newspaperman who had put him on to the hunt in the first place. It was not a terribly long letter, and he smiled sardonically as he read it aloud:

Dear Robert,

By the time you read this, I hope you will have felled the Great Silver Bear of the San Juans in Colorado. If so, my congratulations to you and your party.

Now, as to my small part in bringing all of this about (as you can see, I am optimistic in all things and can only write assuming your success). Perhaps you won't mind doing me a small favor upon your arrival back here in New York, whenever that turns out to be. I would of course love to write another story about the bear, your experiences topping them all. In fact, I am even considering writing a book about it. You, old friend, would quite naturally be welcome to coauthor it and share in the proceeds. So, please be thinking about me and my proposal on your trip back. I am sure we can spend some profitable hours talking about it!

Also, please give my regards to Sir Henry, Lady Gatlin, Lady Greenstreet, Jessica, and Anson (I do hope good old Anson has survived the ordeal!). And do be sure and proffer my best wishes to that one individual to whom I am sure you now owe much of what I pray has been your success, that fine Western outdoorsman and guide, Mr. Dawson Riddle!

> Yours truly,
> Stuart

The members of the group smiled at one another, and the smiles were all wry ones. Dawson, who had taken off on his own shortly after they had arrived back at Gil's ranch, had not been seen since.

"Well, Whitney," Sir Robert said, holding out his hand, "I don't regret even a dollar of what I've paid you for your services. We don't know if we got the bear or not, and I can honestly say that I hope we did not. But I'll tell you for certain, I've never had a bloody experience I'll remember any longer than this one. I hope you can buy some of those cows and things you need now—and, by Jove, I do hope you won't keep that young lass over there waiting much longer to get married. You jolly well could do worse than her, let me tell you!"

June, standing at her mother's side nearby, blushed mightily but did not say a thing.

Gil smiled self-consciously, his eyes fixed on June. "I think you can count on that, Sir Robert. Assuming June is willing to put up with a few hardships yet, out on the ranch. That and Mrs. Greer's blessing, of course."

The older woman's eyebrows raised in mild astonishment. She had—like most others—been quite distraught to hear of Garst Cunningham's demise, but she had proven once more that she was a fair-minded woman when she refused to blame Gil for any of it.

"Gil Whitney, it is June's choice and you know it. You also know that I won't interfere. And if she could stand what she's just

been through, then I'm sure she can weather anything she'll encounter out at that ranch of yours!"

June, still not saying anything, came over to Gil's side and put
an arm around his waist. Her eyes were misted over with what
could only have been tears of sheer happiness. No one needed to
be told what *her* answer would be.

One by one the departing members of the party came up to say
their good-byes. The dapper little Sir Henry stood before Gil, all
smiles and winks and pipe smoke, and said, "By Jove, Whitney, I
missed out on all the fun, didn't I? And I, for one, do wish we'd
brought in that bear. If he's still around, maybe someday I'll come
back. What say to that?" And he winked again as Gil only smiled.

Then came Jessica, tears in her eyes as she first put her arms
around June, then came over to give Gil a light peck on the
cheek.

"I almost fell in love with you, Gil—did you know that? And I
still could, if I stayed long enough and you weren't already taken.
But I've realized something about Anson and myself, too. Who
knows, maybe things will even work out between us now!"

And then there was Anson, shaking hands and smiling, fully
happy for the first time since Gil had known him, followed closely
by Lady Gatlin and Lady Greenstreet, their combined bearing little shaken by the fact that they both were made clearly emotional
by the scene.

Everyone was made emotional: The hunting party, June, Gil,
even Buck and Antonio, who stood close by as the party boarded
the surreys. Fleck, whom Gil had for this one occasion allowed to
come in to town with them, ran and barked in the street. A small
crowd of passersby had formed. A couple of Indian men watched
and nodded their heads from across the street.

And as the caravan moved out and last farewells were called
out, Bud Sampson came over to stand beside Gil and June. He
said, "It was like I said it would be, wasn't it, Gil?"

"And how was that?"

"Something," the storekeeper said sort of proudly. "By golly, it
was really something!"

Gil smiled. "Yeah, I guess it was that, all right. It sure was
that."

The last wagon had just about disappeared around the corner in the street before them as Sampson went on to ask, "What do you think about the bear, Gil? Did he die or not? Will we ever know?"

Gil put an arm around June's shoulders and looked off toward the southeast. The far mountains were mostly hidden by hills that rose just beyond the river, but he could see the distant peaks clearly in his mind's eye just the same. He said, "Unless he shows up again, it could be we never will, Bud. He carried a lot of lead out of that little meadow up there, an awful lot. Tough as he's been, I just don't see how he could have lived through that."

But then he turned back to them, and he was completely unashamed of the slight cracking in his voice as he added, "But you know what? If he were to make it, if I knew for sure that he was still alive out there somewhere and wasn't yet going to die because of what we did to him, I actually think I'd be sort of glad. Yes sir, I actually think I would!"

AFTERWORD

For the time being at least, the storytellers were left to concoct their own endings to this, perhaps the most tantalizing tale about the bear of them all. Some, a few unimaginative realists mostly, insisted that the bear had surely died at those unlikeliest of all hands to ever have a try at him—those of Dawson Riddle, with the help of one of the Englishmen and Gil Whitney, of course. Others—as is the understandable want of real storytellers when dealing with such legends—chose to believe that the bear had survived once more, and would one day emerge to hunt and kill again, just as always had been the case with him before.

Unfortunately for the storytellers, there wasn't a lot to support this latter theory, except that one day about a month after the shooting up in that little meadow, a couple of sheepherders reported the sighting of an unusually large and dark-colored grizzly caught stalking their flocks down near certain headwaters of the Little Navajo River. They got only one quick look—and not even that many shots—at it as it lumbered through the brush to get away after their dogs had barked at it, and they were unable to find a clean forepaw print by which to judge for certain the big animal's identity. But both herders swore that the bear had run rather stiffly, perhaps even with a limp, and that it had looked a bit gaunt, as if it had not been in the best of health recently. They had heard the stories of the shooting of the silver bear earlier in the summer, and quite naturally were quick to speculate that it was *El Oso de Muerte* they had seen.

But was it? They were unable to track the animal and there

were no further sightings reported. That the two sheepherders
were an excitable pair even the most optimistic of the storytellers
had to admit. What they had seen could have been anything from
a very large black bear—unusually dark, was it?—to any size of a
grizzly at all. It could even have been a figment of their imagination, for weren't most sheepherders storytellers also? Maybe they
were like so many others; they simply *wanted* to believe. As quick
as they would have been to fire away at the bear had a good shot
presented itself, they quite conversely did not want their legend to
die. Might they not conjure up almost any kind of sighting to
keep it alive?

Well, maybe so, one storyteller said to another one day. But say
the bear is alive, just say he survived and is right now looking to
make it through another winter. What's it like for him now? How
would you picture it? A time like any other for the bear?

Well . . .

*The waters of the Little Navajo gurgled and rippled half a mile
behind and below him as the big bear dragged a freshly killed
yearling steer up into a favorite daytime lair where he would feed
and sleep and feed again. It was his first such kill in over a month
and would be his first real feast since before he had been shot.
Berries, roots, ants, small mammals, even green grass had been
enough to keep him alive throughout his recovery period, but as
strength returned his craving for red meat had become almost
overpowering.*

*And so at last he had made a kill, at last he would feed. It
would indeed, finally, seem a time like any other for the bear.*

*It had rained the night before; dawn had brought with it crisp
air that was also fresh and clean and clear. The day would eventually become warm, maybe even hot, but for now things were wet
and cool and very pleasant. A time like any other but also a time
of change for the bear.*

*Summer was dragging on; the chokecherries and serviceberries
would soon be gone; fall colors would in but a few weeks come to
dominate the land. The nights, already cool, would soon take on a
sharp chill; early-morning air would be crisp with frost; cattle and
sheep would be moved to lower country and the bear's food sup-*

ply would suddenly become less abundant. He would have to make adjustments all over again, and it might be a bit more difficult this year. Certainly it had not been his easiest summer, this one just passing; it might not be his easiest winter upcoming.

But that didn't mean he could not deal with it. After all, he was the same tough old bear, was he not? What real change had been wrought in him? He had grown a little older, had gained a few more scars and perhaps a permanent limp of sorts, had even come close to dying when the worst of his wounds had been slow to heal. But he had made it, hadn't he? He would keep on making it, would he not?

True, he was no longer a young bear, but he still was not nearly as old as grizzlies sometimes get. Why shouldn't his routine be the same as it always had been? When the first heavy snows arrived and the aspens had fully dropped their leaves, he would return to the basin and make his winter den. He would sleep the dead of winter through, emerge in the spring, forage and mate; perhaps he would even have a fight or two if there were any other grizzlies around that were big enough to challenge him; he would leave his claw marks high up on the trees, higher than any other bear could reach from the ground; he would establish a territory and go on about his business just as he always had before.

Just as he always had before. A time like any other for the silver bear. . . .

And so they told it. The bear, they would have it, was still around; he had survived again and was fully expected to go on surviving. But this didn't mean that people would give up trying to bring him in. It was predictable that for as long as he was known to live, for as long as the stories about him continued to be told, he would be hunted. The lower San Juans were his home, his haven. But they were also where the hunters knew he would be. Not all would be like the Englishman, who came and made his try and, having failed, went away having gained such respect for the beast and its kind that he would never hunt one of them again. Some would be more persistent, and for those who were

M25 not, others would come in their place. More and more, sadly lacking any real stake in whether the animal lived or died, would even come to call it sport.

But for now at least, the bear had weathered the storm: He had defied his enemies and their boom sticks and endless tricks once again. He was still *El Oso de Muerte*—The Bear of Death; he was the Spirit Bear; he was Old Tuffy. Someday, of course, his time would come. But as all who had tried to bring this about thus far would be forced to concede, it wasn't yet. It sure wasn't yet.